MW01122097

the Spiral Maze

the Spiral Maze

Patricia Bow

Thistledown Press Ltd.

© Patricia Bow, 1997

All rights reserved

No part of this publication may be reproduced or transmitted in any form or by any means, electronic or mechanical, including photocopying, recording, or any information storage and retrieval system, without permission in writing from the publisher.

Canadian Cataloguing in Publication Data

Bow, Patricia, 1946 -
The spiral maze
ISBN 1-895449-68-5

I. Title.
PS8553.O8987S75 1997 C813'.54 C97-920045-8
PR9199.3.B68S75 1997

Book design by A.M. Forrie
Cover art by Randy Fogen
Typset by Thistledown Press Ltd.

Printed and bound in Canada by
Veilleux Impression à Demande
Boucherville, Quebec

Thistledown Press Ltd.
633 Main Street
Saskatoon, Saskatchewan
S7H 0J8

Saskatchewan
Arts Board

THE CANADA COUNCIL | LE CONSEIL DES ARTS
FOR THE ARTS | DU CANADA
SINCE 1957 | DEPUIS 1957

We acknowledge the support of the Canada Council for the Arts for our publishing program. Thistledown Press also gratefully acknowledges the continued support of the Saskatchewan Arts Board.

For Eric and James, with love.

Ye who walk these branching ways,
warily and softly wend.
Time and chance make such a maze,
peril lies at every bend.
Here, no hope nor fear is vain.
Here, all dreams may yet come true.
Shades may live, and substance gain;
all things lost be found anew.
Yet wisely tread, or learn the cost:
that finder be forever lost.

One

Neil woke, rising from darkness to darkness. He was lying flat on his back. He couldn't move, he couldn't breathe. Ropes or vines looped tight around his feet and legs, and pinned his arms to his sides.

With a grunt he kicked away the damp sheets and the last of the dream, and sat up. He was sweating and fighting for breath, as if he'd just run a race uphill. The air was warm and thick as soup.

He prodded his groggy brain into gear. *That window must have swung closed again.* He'd had enough trouble prying it open last night and he'd been too tired after the five-hour drive to hunt for something to wedge it with.

He swung his legs off the high bed and slid to the floor. His pyjama bottoms stuck to his sweaty skin. Taking a step into the blackness, his toe slammed into something hard. He crashed, elbows banging on bare floorboards, and lay a moment groaning.

Sitting up, he swept his hands around the dusty floor until he found both his suitcases. He pushed them under the bed so they couldn't ambush him again and stood up, facing the windows.

These were tall casements that opened outward, like doors, and they had no curtains. By a white glow that slanted in from outside, he could see no more booby traps in the way. He could see . . .

Somebody hanging outside the window, looking in.

It was all in black and silver. The two tall windows side by side, with those fantastic onion-shaped arches above, a black outline. They framed a silvery fuzz of distant trees and a shining slice of Lake Huron.

The figure outside the right-hand window was a black silhouette, except for where the moon painted him bright silver: top of head, tip of nose, shoulders, outstretched hand, part of a bent leg.

He was kneeling on the sill and clinging with his left hand to the frame above his head. His right fingertips were moving across the glass as if he was feeling for a way in. He was staring straight at Neil.

Neil's heart hammered twice, and then he was at the window. He grabbed for the latch at the side and twisted. There, locked! This brought him face to face with the cat burglar, if that was what this was.

The tips of their noses were three inches apart. Even in the jigsaw puzzle of moonlight and shadow, he could see the face clearly.

A young face, maybe thirteen. His own age. Black hair cut short. Eyes a glint of silver under straight black brows. Straight nose, straight mouth pressed thin. Skin the colour of moonlight.

It took a moment. Then Neil knew. The knowledge sent a shock wave of blood into his head and out again. He swayed dizzily.

Feature for feature, it was exactly the same as the face he saw in the bathroom mirror every morning.

While he stood gaping, the window frame suddenly emptied itself. Neil shook his head clear, wrenched the latch around and pushed at the casement. This time it flew open so suddenly, he nearly fell out.

There was no screen. He leaned out as far as he dared, expecting to see a body splatted on the brick walkway two storeys below.

No body. But a figure stood in the garden, white face turned up to him above dark clothes. Neil peered down the wall, then left and right, then craned his neck upward. No way. No way at all.

He looked down into the garden again. The boy was gone. Not far, though. He was past the line of lilac trees that edged the garden and was trotting across the meadow of long grass to the south, heading for the ridge. His head turned, he looked back, then he trotted on.

Cool air flooded in through the open window. The air of an August night, smelling of moist leaves and the lake. Neil shivered and realized he was dripping as if he'd been standing in the shower. The waistband of his pyjamas was soaked with sweat.

No wonder, after coming face to face with *that*. He shivered again, and hugged himself.

Then anger swept in, and saved him. Because it wasn't who it looked like, it couldn't have been. As far as he knew, there were only three people in the world who'd ever owned a face like that. His father, for one. Himself, for another. And his twin brother Jasper.

And Jasper had died when he was five days old. Thirteen years ago.

Which meant this guy was a fake.

Not even pausing to find his sneakers, Neil ran out of his room, stood a moment in the dark corridor — which way out? — then remembered that the tower, with its corkscrew staircase, was to his left. In less than a minute he was on his way down, bare feet feeling at the cold brick stairs, one hand on the shaky rail.

At the bottom he slid his hands along the uneven wall till they met wood: the back door. He lost precious moments fumbling for the lock, twisting the thumb latch. Then the door opened with a whoosh of cool air and he was out and running, making up for lost time.

The full moon overhead made it look easy. It wasn't. The colourless light made ditches flatten out and disappear into the grass. Rocks popped into sight suddenly, their black shadows pooled under their feet.

He tripped twice, picked himself up and kept running. Past the lilacs and across the meadow, where the long grass snagged his ankles. Up the hill and into the pines. Dry needles pricked his soles and he smelled resin.

He was warm now with anger, his blood raced. The rougher going didn't slow him much: he only worried he'd be too late to catch up. But when he reached the crest of the ridge he caught sight of a figure in the hollow below, its feet flying silently over the grass. Neil let out a quick, furious laugh and leaped down the slope.

The pines thinned out. The ground dipped, he splashed through a skim of cold water at the bottom, then he was climbing again. The long grassy slope was silver fur in the moonlight. But it had a dark crown.

As Neil's uphill race became a stagger, he saw how big that crown was. Like a fortress. Its walls curved away on both sides toward the lake. He guessed where he was and what he'd found.

The strange boy ran straight uphill, darted through a gap in the wall, and was gone.

Neil reached the spot seconds later, and stood panting. He wasn't fool enough to go rushing into some dark hole after a burglar.

Fool enough to chase him, though. *Why didn't I wake Dad?* But he knew. Seeing that face had driven every other thought out of his head.

His blood was cooling, the excitement draining away with the anger. He took a step nearer to the gap in the hedge.

So this was the maze. It was a place he'd heard of but never seen before. He'd never quite believed it was real. The rare times his father had talked about this place, it had sounded like something out of a fairy tale by the Brothers Grimm.

In fact, all of it — house, maze, family history — still sounded to Neil like a story his father wanted to forget.

The maze was obviously no fiction, though. Here it was, real and solid. Moonlight showed each needle of each sprig of the yew trees that formed it. They made thick, closely trimmed walls right down to the ground, with no thin spots.

The shadow in the gateway was like muddy water. Now that Neil's eyes were more used to the night, he could see something was in there, just beyond the entrance. Waiting. Something moved at waist level. A pointed shape like a snout thrust forward, then it drew back.

Neil shivered again, and not just with cold.

Then came a husky whispering, as if the wind had found a voice. Or many voices.

He backed away, keeping a watch on the gap. *He's trying to scare me off. Don't let him think he's done it. Even if he has.*

"Hey, you!" A good, loud yell, not too high pitched. It rang with confidence. He hoped. "You're on private property!"

A pause to fill the lungs and calm the heartbeat. "You just get out and stay out — you hear?"

No answer, not that he'd expected any. He backed away again until he started to teeter on the slope.

Then he turned and walked with careful dignity downhill to the streamlet and climbed the slope beyond. Invisible eyes swarmed on his back the whole time. The prickly feeling didn't go away until he reached the pines on the ridge and started down again toward the house.

In the garden he felt safe. At least, he didn't feel he'd been followed. He stopped to look up at his bedroom windows.

How had the kid got up there? He didn't have a ladder, he hadn't used a rope. There were no trellises or rainspouts. And the dining room windows, directly below that bedroom, had those same onion-shaped arches, set nearly flush to the stucco. Nothing but a spider could have climbed that wall.

Maybe he flew. Neil chuckled, then hugged his bare arms, all goosebumps. *I must've been crazy!* Craziness ran in the family, if this house was any sign.

He stood grinning up at it, shaking his head. You couldn't take it seriously. A fake Moorish palace, a daydream lifted from the Spain of five hundred years ago and built on the shore of Lake Huron where it had no business to be. So said Dad, who should know, since the house had been in his family for a hundred and fifty years.

Stucco gleaming white in the moonlight, chimneys disguised as minarets. Rows of arched windows set off by marble columns. Curly lattice trim along the edge of the flat roof and between the windows and anywhere else there was an inch of space.

And most fantastic of all, the tower, rising from the rear of the house, its pale green copper dome bleached by the moon.

In the moonlight, in fact, the building looked unreal. As if at any moment it might float up and skim away like a magic carpet. The sight was so dreamlike that Neil thought: That's it! Of course! I'm dreaming.

He lightened all over with relief. The wall-climber with *that face* had to be part of the dream.

Stumbling, exhausted, shivering, he found his way indoors and up the dark stairs again, and climbed into bed.

♋

Hunger woke him next morning. According to his watch, which he'd left on the twisty-legged little table beside his bed, it was 8:02. The arched windows framed bright blue sky.

He sat up, blinking, and a zigzag of pine tops came into view. The dream was still with him, all its details vivid. Neil hardly ever remembered his dreams.

He stretched his arms above his head and smiled at the weirdness of it. A burglar who swarmed up walls like a spider!

"Time to get up, I guess."

He moved his feet, and made a face. Felt like there was grit on the sheets. Funny, they'd been clean last night. Throwing back the top sheet, he stared. Brown marks on the white cotton. Greenish stains on the knees of his pyjamas. And his feet . . .

He was afraid to look. When he pulled them out, flakes of dried mud and blades of grass fell from between his toes.

He rolled out of bed and ran to the window.

The casement had swung closed again. The sun was rising on the other side of the house, but on this side the light was bright enough to show a veil of dust over the outside of the glass. It probably hadn't been cleaned since Aunt Esther died, six months ago.

And across the pane, where the dream-boy's fingers had moved, ran a line of letters. Big, straggly capitals drawn in the dust.

CHARLOTTE NEEDS HELP TELL FLEUR HURRY JASPER

Two

Jasper.

Next instant Neil was on his knees, eyes an inch from the glass, his fingers tracing the letters, as if that would help him make sense of things. Then, angrily, he pushed himself away from the window.

"Wake up! There's got to be more than one person in the world named Jasper!"

With that face? muttered a quiet voice in the back of his mind. The right age, too. And it wasn't a dream, because there on the window was the proof.

"Yeah, sure. Only it just can't be."

He swung away from the window, then turned back. One other thing had just struck him. The printing was on the dusty outside of the glass, yet seen from the inside, it was the right way around. This "Jasper" would have had to write backwards. Now, there was a trick not everybody could do.

The whole thing was so crazy, Neil didn't know whether to laugh it off or punch the wall. Being Neil, he just stood quietly and let the questions boil around in his mind.

Who was this stranger and what was he up to? Who was Fleur? Who was Charlotte? He took a last look at the message in the dust and saw another line of letters under the first. A short line, and faint, as if the writing fingers had grown tired.

PADGETT, it said.

Padgett who?

An idea surfaced from the boiling and struck Neil on the forehead. For a moment he stood with his mouth open. Then he laughed. Of course! The answer was so obvious, he wanted to kick himself for not seeing it right away.

He didn't bother washing. The idea was too important. He dragged his suitcases out from under the bed, found socks and underwear, black jeans and plain white T-shirt, shoved feet into sneakers.

Leaving the suitcases open on the floor, he made for the tower at the back of the house. From the landing, stairs of yellow-grey brick twisted up to the right and down to the left.

He hadn't had a chance yet to see what was at the top of the tower. *Better be careful when I do.* The edges of the steps were crumbling. One brick cracked as he stepped on it.

"It's a miracle I didn't kill myself last night!"

He found his father in the kitchen, lining up objects on the counter in front of him. Two cans of tomato soup, a box of salt and a jar with a few tea bags in it.

"That's it. There's our breakfast."

It sounded like one of Gregory's dry jokes. Neil ignored it and plunged right into his question.

"Dad! Our family came here from Scotland, right? Dexter Gunn and his family, I mean. When? How long have we been here?"

"They came to this area in 1843." Gregory walked to the refrigerator, opened it and inspected the shining emptiness inside. "Why the sudden interest?"

"Well, if the family's lived around Amstey for so many years, I must have a lot of relatives here. Like, cousins I don't know about. Some my own age, maybe."

"No." The fridge door thudded shut. "I'm sorry if you were looking forward to finding cousins. We're not a prolific family." As he spoke he crossed to the windows, another set of

Arabian-nights arches, and thumped a casement open with
the heel of his hand. Morning air gushed in from the courtyard, smelling of cut grass and damp stone.

With the window open and the light on, it should have
been a cheery room. The floor was brick, set in a zigzag
pattern. The big pine table in the middle was just begging
to be loaded with a sizzling breakfast.

But the floor was so cold, Neil could feel it right through
his sneaker soles. And even with the lights on, the room was
dim. He rubbed his arms and shivered.

"Dad, there must be some cousins. There's got to be at
least . . . " He knew this sounded strange. His father was
giving him a slant-headed look. "At least one who looks like
me," he ended.

"Well, there isn't. It's just you and me, kid."

"Then something really weird is going on." He took a
deep breath and told the story. Just the facts, no embroidery.
Even to him it sounded like the meanderings of a sleep-fogged
brain.

"Some dream," Gregory said, smiling.

"I wasn't asleep. And I can prove it!"

His father shrugged, but followed him upstairs. "He wrote
on the glass," Neil threw back over his shoulder as he bounded
along the upstairs hall, the wooden floor squeaking at every
step. "On the outside. I couldn't possibly have . . . "

He pushed open the bedroom door and crossed to the
window. Then stood staring at the sparkling glass. Not a trace
of dust on it. His father reached from behind him and pushed
the casement open. A drop of water clung to the bottom
edge.

"It's been washed." Neil pushed the casement open wide
and leaned out. The end of a ladder was swinging around
the front corner of the house. "Who was that?"

"The lawyer hired some local company to keep the place in trim till the will's settled." Gregory grabbed him by the arm and pulled him back in. "I guess that's them."

"Dad, I wasn't dreaming. Look!" He dashed to the bed and flung back the cover to show the grimy sheets.

"That does prove you were out last night. But the rest . . . " He shook his head slowly. Neil wilted. *I wasn't dreaming*, he insisted silently, but he didn't bother saying it again.

Gregory stared at him a moment longer, with his eyebrows knotted together. Then he gave Neil a gentle push towards the door. "Come on. We've got business in town."

They crunched down the crumbling brick steps, both too busy watching where they put their feet to talk. When they reached the bottom of the stairs, Gregory stopped and looked up. Neil looked up too. The stairs corkscrewed up into shadow.

He held his breath. Was that a footstep above them?

No. Just a whisper, wind through cracked casements.

Gregory gave himself a shake, and laughed. "Something in the structure, maybe . . . "

"What is?"

"Oh, there were always stories about this place. And it didn't help being a member of the family. When I was a kid I had to come here once a month, with my mother and father."

"What for?"

Gregory reached for the door handle. "It was a kind of duty. My parents sat in the parlour and paid their respects to Aunt Esther, who was a thousand years old even then, and I roamed around the place. Never roamed far, though. It's a big old house, and it's creakier than most. Easy to imagine you hear things."

And I wasn't imagining things last night, either, Neil thought back at him. Aloud he said, "What stories?"

"Never mind. We both have to sleep here."

"Thanks, Dad. Thanks a lot."

Gregory laughed and waved Neil out the open door.

♋

They followed the brick paving around to the front of the house, where they'd left the car, and climbed in. Gregory steered slowly around the circular drive.

Off to the right, a flicker caught Neil's eye. A man in dark green overalls lifted garden shears and snipped at the lilac hedge, and the blades flashed in the morning sun.

Neil stared at him through the rolled-down window. The guy was funny looking, as if somebody'd got the measurements wrong before they put him together. Too short in the legs, too big across the shoulders, with a small, round head hidden under a peaked cap. Thick gloves covered his hands.

Just as the driveway curved in among the trees that separated the Gunn property from the highway, Neil looked back one last time. The man was standing perfectly still. Except for his head, which turned slowly to watch the car out of sight.

Neil shrugged off the notion that the gardener had been watching him, in particular. Not the car, not Gregory, but him. That was sheer itchy nervousness. *He doesn't know me from a hole in the ground!*

The drive to town wasn't long. Ten minutes south on Highway 21, with Lake Huron glittering on their right and fields of ripe corn on the left, divided by fences of rock and timber.

Gregory pointed out a hill rising ahead of them, near the lake. "There it is. Amstey. Or at least the residential part. Some nice Victorian houses up there on Sentinel Hill. The downtown's on the flats, to the south."

A church spire topped with a glinting cross thrust up among the trees on the hill crest. Amstey looked like a nice place to live.

"Why did old Dexter build his house so far out of town?" Neil asked. "Was he some kind of hermit?"

"No, he just thought he was a cut above the other settlers." As Amstey reached out curving roads like long arms to gather them in, Gregory talked about the town's peculiar street plan, which was the pride of the locals and a joke to everyone else.

Reaching the centre of town, they turned left onto Queen's Circle, then drove around the circular roadway until they found a parking spot. They got out and stood looking around.

"That's the town hall." Gregory pointed at a huge granite pile in the middle. Shops of brick and stone lined the roadway facing it, cosily shoulder to shoulder. Maple and chestnut trees half buried them in green.

There were no crowds, and none of the people who strolled along looked busy. It was so different from downtown Toronto, where Neil had grown up, that it might as well have been a town in a foreign country.

Gregory cleared his throat. "Like it? It's usually described as Dexter's crude attempt to outdo Goderich."

"Dexter? Outdo? I don't get it."

"Goderich has a street plan based on an octagon, an eight-sided figure, remember?" Gregory drew lines in the air. He was an engineer, he knew these things. "All the downtown streets radiate out from that centre like the spokes of a wheel."

Neil stared around the circle of buildings, then saw. "And Amstey has a circle in the middle and curving streets instead of straight ones. But you said — Dexter? You mean he — "

"Designed the town? Sure."

"How come I never knew that?"

"I'm sure I told you, one time or another. If it didn't sink in, it must be that you were never interested before."

"Well, now I am. Why've I've never been here before?"

"Face it, you'd have been bored. Speaking of boredom, you have a choice. Come with me to see the lawyer and the real estate agent, or amuse yourself for an hour or so."

"I . . . " Neil's eyes swept around the circle of shop fronts again, then fixed.

"Neil?"

"I . . . I'll be okay on my own."

"All right." Gregory dug in his pocket for his wallet. "Have some breakfast. This should cover it." He held out a ten-dollar bill.

"What about you?"

"I'll be back at the car at . . . " A glance at his watch. "High noon. Then we'll shop for groceries and maybe see a bit of the countryside. How's that for a plan?"

"Sounds good to me."

Neil watched his father vanish up a side street, then he took another look around the circle. The shop he'd spotted was a third of the way around. It was hard to be sure at this distance, but the word on the sign looked a lot like PADGETT.

He held his breath a moment. Padgett, last seen written in dust on his window. This had to mean something. But what?

One thing he was sure of. Jasper wasn't alive. He'd died thirteen years ago. Yet somebody who went by that name was wearing the face Jasper would have worn if he'd lived: Neil's face, too. And lurking outside Neil's window by moonlight.

He set off around the circle at a fast, angry walk. Something screwy was going on here. It was like a cryptic crossword, the kind he liked, because they were harder.

He was good at them, too. He meant to solve this one if it took him the rest of the summer.

♋

A red neon outline of a steaming cup of coffee hung in
PADGETTS' front window. Neil pulled open the door and
walked in. A bell jangled overhead. Inside, the shop smelled
of coffee, chocolate and apple cider. His stomach rumbled. He
figured it must have shrunk to the size of a pea.

He was almost the only customer, maybe because it was
early. Aside from two women drinking tea near the front, the
white iron tables and chairs were empty.

The walls were lined with shelves loaded with fancy tea
canisters and coffee makers, and behind the shelves were
mirrors. He guessed that was to make the place look bigger,
because it couldn't have been more than twenty feet wide.

At the far end of the room, behind the counter, a girl was
standing with her back to him. She was piling icing-covered
cinnamon buns into a pyramid on a plate. Each time she
moved a bun she licked her fingers.

She looked around and smiled cheerfully. "Hi there!"

As Neil walked toward her, he caught sight of his reflection
stalking along on the other side of the shelves. For a few
seconds he played the mirror game. He imagined his twin
was there, walking with him side-by-side.

It was a game he'd played a lot when he was small. Not
lately, though. He knew it was wishful thinking, and he'd
grown out of it.

The girl popped the last bun on top of the pyramid, licked
her fingers one more time, then twirled around to face him.

"What can I do for you?"

"I'd like some breakfast. Got anything besides those buns?"

Her eyebrows went up. "They're delicious. My dad baked
them, and he's the best baker in town. Try one!"

"No, thanks." He glanced at her hands. He expected her
to look embarrassed, but she just grinned.

"My mouth is germ free, like a dog's."

She was his age or close to it, and about as tall. Her thick brown hair was studded with barrettes and combs with gold stars and moons jiggling on them.

The barrettes weren't much use. Her hair kept sliding over her face and she kept pushing it back. A gold chain with an oval pendant on it swung from her left wrist.

She made Neil think of one of those mobiles they hang over babies' cribs, always in motion. Now she was up on her toes, peering over his shoulder.

"What the heck is that?"

He turned quickly, just in time to see a black, pointy-eared shape with the sun behind it pressing its face against the window. It stood too high for a dog, but there was nothing else it could be.

Neil felt chilled, the way he had last night outside the maze. This time he felt a strong urge to duck behind the counter, where the dog couldn't see him.

Next moment it dropped from sight.

Wimp! he sneered at himself. He made a point of turning his back on the window.

As he turned, he caught another glimpse of his reflection in one of the mirrors.He was startled to see himself looking so aghast and sickly-pale. He stepped closer.

His reflection's lips started moving. *Look out*, it mouthed. *Danger.*

Neil stood perfectly still.

Then a shiver passed over the glass as if it were water and his normal face glared back at him, mouth open in shock.

Three

The girl dashed around the counter, grabbed Neil by an arm and pushed him down into the nearest chair. He gave his head a shake and blinked up at her.

"You were going to faint. What is it, don't you eat enough?" She looked him over. "You're as thin as an alleycat!"

"FLEUR!" bellowed a man's voice from somewhere in the back of the shop. She made a face, turned and slouched through a door behind the counter.

Fleur, Neil thought. And this is Padgett's coffee shop. *Fleur Padgett.* He got up, still feeling woozy, and walked to the end of the counter. Through the half-open door beyond came the banging of pots, the shriek of a blender, and bits of sentences.

" . . . not to bother the customers!" The man's voice.

" . . . don't let me do *anything!*" Fleur, complaining.

"When you're older." A woman's voice.

Then brisk footsteps and the woman came out, smiling and tying on a red apron with *Padgetts'* embroidered across the top.

Neil ordered two scones with butter and honey, and a glass of chocolate milk. The tea-drinking women left and he was alone in the coffee shop. He kept his eyes on the white enamel table top and away from the mirrors and the window.

So he'd found one part of his puzzle. Fleur. Now, how to find out what she knew?

Fleur sauntered in from the back as he was wolfing down the second scone. Over her jeans she was wearing a black T-shirt with a map of the solar system printed on it in silver.

"That's the worst of being the youngest in the family," she said. "Or second youngest. They think you can't do anything right! They keep telling you to stop whatever you're doing."

"Big family?" he prompted.

She slid into a chair, put her elbows on the table and held a hand up to tick the fingers. "Well, there's my parents and me and Gran and my brother Richard. They all keep the shop running. Then there's Elaine and her husband Carl and Piglet . . . "

"Who?"

"Alexander." She grinned. "My sister Elaine's baby. He's fat and pink and he eats all the time, so he's Piglet. Then there's my other sister Betts. All together we're nine in the house."

"Nine!" He could hardly imagine it.

She laughed. "Yeah, it's a squeeze. I have to share with Betts. Why, how many's at your house?"

"Two."

"Only two? Mother or father?"

"Father," he said coldly.

Her mouth opened and he knew it was to ask where his mother was, but then her eyes flickered and she just said, "Hm. If your dad's like you, it must be a quiet place."

He cleared his throat. "And Jasper? Where does he fit in?"

"Who's Jasper?"

"You don't know a Jasper?" He tried not to sound as suspicious as he felt.

"Never heard of him."

"Or a Charlotte?"

"Well, of course I know about Charlotte!"

"Aha." He set down his milk glass and sat forward. "Tell me about her, then."

She stared at him. "You are so strange. Where you from?"

"Toronto. But my dad was born here. Now, about Char —"

"Are you on your holidays?"

"Sort of. Mainly we're here to see about our house. About selling it, I mean. My great-aunt left it to my dad. But who on earth would want to buy a dump like that, way out there — "

"You don't mean the old Gunn house!" She sat straight up. When he nodded, she jumped out of her chair. "Mom! Dad!" she shrieked.

They were there in moments, first her father rubbing dough from his fingers, then her mother and a tall boy who turned out to be Richard, pencil and clipboard in hand.

When they found out he was old Esther Gunn's grand-nephew, they made a fuss over him. Mr. Padgett said the food and drink were on the house, Richard went to the cash register and gave him his money back, and Mrs. Padgett hugged him.

Neil wasn't used to being hugged, especially not like this. It was like being cornered by a talcum-scented steamroller. He tried not to show how smothered he felt, but after he freed himself, he saw Fleur giggling at him.

Her mother kept shaking her head in wonder. "And your father? He's well? Goodness, twenty years! My, but you have the look of him. He was the handsomest boy in school."

Her father boomed, "So this is your first visit, Neil? Why on earth haven't you been to Amstey before this?"

"I've wondered that myself."

"Well, now! Fleur, why don't you show Neil around the town?" Mrs. Padgett picked two cinnamon buns off the platter, handed one to each of them, and gave them a gentle push toward the door. "Go on, kids, enjoy yourselves."

♋

"And way up there, see?" Fleur pointed north along Simcoe Street, to the slopes of Sentinel Hill. "See at the top, the spire? That's the church of St. Michael and All Angels. There's a little park right on the hilltop and the church is on one side, and our house is on the other. See that shine in the trees?"

Neil squinted at it. "Okay."

"That's my skylight. Dad put it in so the attic wouldn't seem so closed-in over my head."

"You sleep in an attic?"

"Sure! It's fixed up, of course. With nine people in the house, every inch counts. I'll bet that would drive you crazy." Her round blue eyes were as innocent as a baby's, but he knew she was laughing at him. Oddly, he didn't mind.

Fleur wasn't the kind of girl he liked to spend time with, at least he'd never have thought so before now. Five minutes in the same room with her would've had him climbing the walls. She talked too much and she never just walked: she bounced or danced or darted. It was hard to think with her around.

But as they wandered along the curving streets, Neil felt for the first time as if he really was on holiday.

The sun shone hot. The breeze whipped Fleur's hair into her eyes, snapped awnings up and down, and dried the sweat on Neil's neck. The brick and stone buildings had a comfortable, old-shoe look, even the biggest, which was all of four storeys high, and topped with a fancy stone cornice.

And the cinnamon buns were delicious, oozing butter from their crumbling folds. You had to be quick with your tongue if you didn't want to lose any of it.

Fleur showed him all her favourite stores. Most of them sold used books or old clothes. Every time they stopped to look in a store window, Neil watched his reflection for signs it would start to move on its own, but it never did. Little by little, he relaxed.

Once he saw the man in the green overalls slouching along behind them, about two stores distant. Feeling friendly, Neil waved, but the man just ducked his head and turned away. A real ray of sunshine. Neil shrugged and forgot him.

"Believe it or not, I'm starting to think you're okay, Neil." Fleur licked the last smear of icing from her fingers. "I'm glad you came into the coffee shop with your crazy questions. You're all I've got."

"Got?" he repeated warily.

"My one best friend's at this expensive summer camp with horses. And my other best friend moved to Edmonton with her family. And Mom and Dad say I'm too young to help out at the coffee shop. All I've got to do is babysit Piglet."

They ran to catch the next green light, then Fleur pulled him to a stop in front of a window labelled ANTIQUES, in gold letters. The sun sparkled on cracked tea cups, brass door-knockers and tarnished silver jewellery set with dark red and purple stones, or maybe they were just glass.

Fleur pressed her nose to the window and fogged it with her breath. "I love this place! I love all these strange old things."

Neil wasn't impressed. "Just a lot of worn-out stuff. Some of it, you can't even tell what it's for."

"But those are the best things! Because they could be for *anything*, don't you see? You could even imagine they were magic. Like my moonstone."

She held up her left wrist, to show the pendant hanging on a gold chain. It was a pearly oval the size of a thumbnail, set in a plain gold frame.

"So you believe in magic?" Neil managed not to laugh. He turned the stone in his fingers and saw curly threads glowing in the milky depths. They looked like the loops of a fingerprint.

Fleur's cheeks reddened. "I didn't say that! I said you could *imagine* it was magic. For fun. Actually I'm not even sure what kind of stone it is. Mr. Venables in there," she nodded into the shop, "doesn't know either. It might only be quartz. But I found it, so it's my lucky piece even if it isn't magic, or a moonstone or anything precious. I wear it all the time, day and night."

Neil usually found jewellery boring, so his own interest in this pendant surprised him. It must be unusual. It felt even more interesting than it looked. Under his fingertips it was warm and silky, yet his nail found it hard.

"Hey." Fleur pulled her wrist away and nudged him. "D'you know those guys?"

"Who?" Neil looked around and saw the man standing in the doorway of the hardware store, just a few yards away. It was the gardener he'd waved at earlier. His cap was pulled low over his eyes and he seemed to be interested in something inside the store. He still wore those thick gloves.

On the other side of him, almost hidden, was another man in the same green overalls, cap and gloves. Must be a uniform, Neil thought. They must both work for the same company.

"I looked up," Fleur muttered, "and he was staring straight at me. Or maybe at both of us."

With collars up and hats pulled right down over the ears, it was hard to see either man's face. And both their mouths were closed so tight, they almost didn't have mouths.

"Neil, who are they?"

"I don't know."

Suddenly the nearest man turned from the hardware store and started slowly toward them. The second man followed.

They had the same odd, strutting walk, not clumsy exactly, but as if their knees didn't work properly.

A heavy lump formed in the pit of Neil's stomach, and it got heavier as the two stalked nearer. He felt their eyes on his face and wanted to hide.

"How weird," Fleur whispered. "They know you."

"I think . . . I don't want to meet them." Neil ducked inside the antique store, with Fleur at his heels. Brass chimes swung and clanged as the door closed.

A small man with hardly any hair was sitting at a richly carved and very cluttered desk. A pair of steel-rimmed glasses, their lenses dull with dust, rode low on his nose. He smiled at them over the top. "How are you, Fleur? Come to browse?"

"I . . . uh, Mr. Venables, I've got someone for you to meet." She grabbed Neil's elbow and pushed him forward. "Neil Gunn. In fact," she added with a flourish in her voice, "I guess you could call him the last of the Gunns."

"The last of Dexter's line. This is exciting!" Mr. Venables rose and pattered forward, hand outstretched. "I've heard you're going to sell that wonderful house. What about the furnishings? Will they be sold separately? If so, I'd . . . "

"I — I don't know. Sorry. I'll tell my father you were asking." Neil glanced back over his shoulder. The gardeners were standing outside the window, looking in. They began shuffling toward the door.

"Is there another way out?" Neil demanded.

Mr. Venables stared at him, then at the door. "Why on earth?"

As the door handle turned, Fleur took over. "Looks like we got to run, I'll be back, 'bye!"

Her hand still tight on Neil's elbow, she rushed him around the small man, along an aisle with old dressers and cupboards towering on each side, and out into a dusty area full of wooden boxes. Here they found a double set of scarred and dirty doors.

The doors opened on a shadowy brick alley between the backs of shops. Fleur turned right, then stopped short. Neil bumped into her. "No way," she said. "How'd he get out there so fast?"

The end of the alley was a slot full of sun. A hunched silhouette stood against the brightness. It flashed Neil a sudden memory of the dog shape that had looked at him through the window of the coffee shop.

But this was unmistakably a man, not a dog. Neil didn't understand why he felt so cold, or why the prickly feet of warning were crawling all over his neck.

Four

Come on!" Fleur waved at him from a gap in the wall opposite the back of the antique shop. He followed her and found a crack, barely wide enough to squirm through, between two brick buildings.

It led into a backyard wilderness of long grass, scrub maples, thistles and purple phlox. Midges rose in clouds as they ran through. Fleur crawled between the broken boards of a fence.

Then, unexpectedly, they stood on the bank of a stream. The backs of houses rose on the other bank, ten yards away. Lawns sloped down to the water, their swing sets and barbecues looking comfortingly normal. Around a bend to the left glittered the lake.

"That'll hold 'em. They won't follow us through there!" Fleur plumped down in the long grass. Neil collapsed with a sigh of relief beside her. He remembered his earlier thought that she'd drive him up the wall in five minutes, and took it back.

"Y'know, you're not so bad yourself."

She looked surprised. "What's this?"

"Most people would have been all over me, asking questions, getting in the way. You just took off!"

"Well, I could see you were spooked. Who *are* those guys?"

"They work for a company that takes care of people's property. One was at our house this morning." He frowned. "Or maybe the other was there too and I just didn't see him.

I think they're following me, but don't ask me why." He pulled at a big purple thistle and yelped when it pricked him.

"Funny how much they look alike. You notice?" She fingered her pendant thoughtfully.

"I noticed. Hey! Maybe they're brothers." He sat up straight, relieved. That explanation made the gardeners seem much less sinister.

"The Ugly Brothers?" Fleur laughed. Then she shook her head. "No. It's more than just a family likeness, they're like Xerox copies of each other. They are definitely weird!"

The stream chuckled and glinted in front of them. Small shadows darted under the glitter. Neil watched the minnows and tried to see his next move.

He thought of the maze, and how the so-called Jasper had escaped into it, and his pulse quickened. Maybe, inside, he'd find some trace.

Fleur nibbled a blade of grass, then tossed it into the water. "Answer time, Neil. What's going on?"

"Going on?" What could he possibly say, that she'd believe? There was no way he could tell her what he'd seen last night, or why he'd come looking for her. But he couldn't let her slip away, either. She was his only lead.

"Don't act dumb." She poked his arm. "You came to the coffee shop looking for somebody."

"I'm looking for Charlotte. You said you knew her."

"Charlotte?" She narrowed her eyes at him as if she wasn't sure of his mental health.

"I guess you think I've been acting nuts." He tried a careless laugh. "I . . . I've got a lot on my mind, that's all. It would help if you'd tell me about Charlotte."

She stared at him a moment longer, then shrugged. "You must have heard some of it from your dad. No? Nothing about how your great-great-great — I don't know how many greats — uncle fell in love with my same-number-of-greats aunt, and ran off with her?"

He shook his head, totally lost.

"Dexter." She prodded his arm again. "The one who built that house of yours. The one who started this town. It all happened a hundred years ago. Or more. Gran told me all about it. They'd been, you know, *courting* and then, for no reason, they just disappeared together! Nobody ever saw them again. She was only eighteen. Isn't it just like a mystery story?"

"What are you talking about?"

"Charlotte," she said impatiently. "My Charlotte who ran off with your Dexter. Got it now?"

"But that's ancient history!"

"That's what I'm *telling* you!"

"Then it's no use to me at all. I'm not interested in the past. Don't you know any other Charlottes?"

"No, I don't. Why? What's this all about?"

"I don't know what it's all about. And that's the truth," he added as she turned on him fiercely. He stood up, slapping dust from his jeans. "Thanks for trying to help."

"Oh, no. You think this is goodbye, don't you? You don't get rid of me that easy." She bounced to her feet. A barrette slipped and swung on the end of a strand of hair. She ignored it.

"I'm not trying to get — "

"Yes, you are. But I told you I like strange things." She flashed a smile. "And you're strange, Neil. Whatever you're up to, I'm in on it." She caught the barrette and refastened it.

Neil's instinct rebelled. He wasn't a pack animal, he was used to working out problems on his own.

On the other hand, the message on the glass had named Fleur, along with Charlotte. *Tell Fleur.*

Besides, odd as it might be, he liked Fleur. And he owed her one for helping him give the Ugly Brothers the slip.

"Well, since you're already mixed up in it," he began.

"Sh!" She touched his arm. He paused and listened. Something rustled in the grass on the other side of the fence. They heard the squeak of dry wood moving on a nail. It might only be a cat, but . . . Neil's neck prickled again.

Fleur turned and picked her way quietly along the stream bank. After five minutes the backyard wilderness to their left drew back, and they were walking along a strip of trimmed parkland. The stream banks flared out like a trumpet and became lake shore. Glassy waves lifted and shattered at their feet.

"What next, Neil?"

"You're not letting it drop, are you?"

"Nope. You're my summer project."

"Okay, then. Next, the maze. You want — "

"To explore it?" She cut him off excitedly. "Are you kidding? I've always wanted to explore it. Who wouldn't?"

"You mean you never have?"

"It's on private land. The one time we — me and my friends — biked up there to try it, the old lady chased us off. Sorry, I mean your great-aunt. She yelled something about how it was dangerous, but of course we didn't believe her."

"Well, nobody'll chase you off now. You can explore it with me. If you like."

"If I like!" Fleur did a little dance on the damp sand. "When?"

"Today? After supper? I have some things to do first with my dad," he added. "And I'd better rent a bike. I can't expect him to drive me back and forth all the time."

"Never mind renting, you can borrow Rick's. He never uses it, not since he got his red Corvette."

"You sure?" It seemed to Neil she was being awfully free with her brother's belongings.

"He won't care. Come on, let's go see if the tires need filling."

As they walked north toward Sentinel Hill, they watched for a pair of short-legged, hump-shouldered figures. But the Uglies — he couldn't help thinking of them that way — were nowhere to be seen.

"You know," Fleur said, "they probably just wanted to pass a message on to your dad. Like, about the garden."

That sounded so obvious, Neil's neck grew hot. He'd made a complete fool of himself over nothing.

"All the same, I'm glad we never came face to face," he said defiantly. "Let them use the phone like anybody else. They give me the creeps."

♋

The maze on its hill was a whaleback of darkness under a butter-yellow sky.

"It's too quiet," Fleur whispered dramatically as she climbed. "It's spooky!"

Neil laughed. "You wish."

Fleur laughed too, but he could tell she'd only been half joking. It *was* too quiet near the maze.

The sun had set and the wind had fallen. A creak of crickets broke the stillness, but that was all. The long grass on the hill stood motionless. Fleur had changed to khaki shorts because it was still so warm, and the bristly stems of corn-flowers whipped her bare knees.

"Your Dexter really . . . made sure," Fleur said jerkily as she climbed, "that . . . nobody was going to see the maze from . . . above, didn't he? That way . . . nobody could . . . cheat!"

Neil stopped and looked around, swinging his nylon gym bag. "I see what you mean." He pointed south. "Those sand hills are between us and the town. Even from the church spire, using binoculars, you couldn't see the maze, let alone see in."

"And that ridge with the pines hides us from the house. And there's trees between us and the highway." She pointed her chin east. "I can't hear any cars."

And to the west, below the bluff, stretched the lake, the same bright gold as the sky.

"You've just explained why it's so quiet," Neil said. "We're sheltered."

It was a sensible explanation. But it didn't stop him from feeling that the nearest other human was a thousand miles away.

The walls of yew seemed to grow higher as they climbed nearer. When at last they stood beside the maze, looking up, the hedge towered over them. Neil jumped, reaching, and fell back after grazing the top with his fingers.

"A good eight feet!"

Fleur looked uneasily at the dimness inside the entrance. "We shouldn't have left it so late."

"Don't worry. We've got a half hour of light left. And even after it gets dark, we'll have no trouble seeing these."

He unzipped the gym bag and pulled out a plastic bag full of white marbles. "Or this." He held up a roll of white twine. "Bought them this afternoon. You see, it pays to think ahead." He smiled as he zipped up the bag.

"Don't be so pleased with yourself. I still say it's too dark."

Neil knew he'd left it too late, but he didn't want to admit he'd made a mistake. "Not scared, are you?" he asked casually.

It was the very thing to spur her on. "Let's go!" she snapped, and flung herself at the gap.

Next moment she was rolling in the grass, clutching her shin.

"What happened?" Neil dropped to his knees beside her.

"Rock!" she said from between clenched teeth. She sat up, gave her bruised shin a rub, then crawled over to the patch of long grass she'd tripped on. The grass hid a small boulder with a metal plate bolted to one smoothed face.

"Look, there's writing on this." Neil peered over her head. Green oxide and stars of brownish lichen made the engraved letters hard to read, especially in the hazy light of evening.

Fleur ran her fingertips over the plate. "'Ye who walk these . . . branching ways,'" she read, "'war . . . warily and softly wend.' What the heck?"

"Branching ways? It's about the maze! I guess Dexter put it there. Advice to the visitor, sort of. What else does it say?"

Fleur crouched over the stone, mumbling to herself. Then she read aloud, slowly:

> Ye who walk these branching ways,
>   warily and softly wend.
> Time and chance make such a maze,
>   peril lies at every bend.
> Here, no hope nor fear is vain.
> Here, all dreams may yet come true.
> Shades may live, and substance gain;
>   all things lost be found anew.
> Yet wisely tread, or learn the cost:
>   that finder be forever lost.

Neil and Fleur knelt in silence while a little of the light drained from the sky and the darkness deepened in the maze. *Lost*, hissed a tiny breeze in the yew thickets.

"Cheerful!" Fleur straightened up.

"Well, it does mention dreams coming true."

"Also perils. That's dangers, right? And what's all that about shades?"

"It's just a poem. It doesn't have to make sense."

Five

Inside the entrance the way branched in three directions: left, right and straight ahead.

"Let's try the middle path." Neil pulled out a bag of marbles and ripped the end off. He bent and set one at the side of the path he'd chosen. It made a clear dot of white on the dark turf.

"This is a system I've read about, in case you're wondering. Puzzles are kind of my hobby. Good thing those gardeners keep the path trimmed."

He glanced at Fleur, but she didn't look impressed. "And the string? Is that another system?"

"That's to mark our way once we've found it." He tied the end of the twine to a wiry branch and handed the roll to Fleur. "Here. Let it out as we go along. Keep it about elbow high and sort of rest it in among the sprigs."

After a few minutes' walking between the curving leafy walls, they came to another branch. "Left this time, okay?" He took another marble from his bag and set it down in the path behind them. Then he placed another at the side of the path they were entering. He looked at Fleur. "You get it?"

She was looping the twine around a spray of needles, to keep it level. "Of course I get it! It doesn't take a brain surgeon to figure it out," she said crossly. "You put down a marble every time we leave a path or start a new one. That way you can tell where we've been."

"Right. You see, we can't get lost. Each time we come to a place where the path branches, we choose a branch we haven't tried before."

"Wonderful," Fleur muttered.

As they set off again, walking quickly, he wondered why she was so grumpy all of a sudden. "Turn right," he said. "Stuffy in here, isn't it?"

"Mph."

"Right again. Might as well explore this whole corner. Still lots of string?"

"Mm."

"Are you okay? You look a bit pale."

"I'm fine!" she snarled.

Neil peered at her. Her face was ghost white in the gloom. He decided he'd better just leave her alone.

Overhead, the dark yew walls towered higher, leaned closer, filling the air with their dusty and bitter scent.

"Nearly there," he said, more cheerfully than he felt. "Notice how the curves are getting tighter? I think we're close to the centre."

Then the walls vanished from either side. Fleur took three wobbly steps into the sudden open space, threw back her head and spread her arms. She stood breathing deeply, while Neil stared at her.

"Come on, it wasn't that bad," he said.

"For me it was."

The space was oval, about ten feet by twelve, and empty except for a wooden bench and a water fountain built of smooth beach stones. Fleur collapsed onto the bench.

"I should've known better," she muttered. "No, how could I've known? I thought, under the open sky like that . . . " She wiped sweat from her cheek with the back of her hand.

"What are you mumbling about?"

"You wouldn't understand."

"You could at least try me."

"Well . . . " She ran a hand through her hair, knocked a comb into the grass and bent to pick it up. "Claustrophobia!" she announced, and gave him a look that dared him to laugh.

"What? You mean, you're afraid . . . "

"Of closed-in places. Yeah."

Neil gave his head a shake. Perhaps because she wasn't afraid of the Uglies, it surprised him to find she was afraid of anything at all. "You're kidding."

"Oh, it's not like I run screaming from elevators, just . . . " She dug the comb back in place. "Well, it's healthier to take the stairs anyway, right?"

"I *thought* something was wrong, back there. Why didn't you tell me?"

"It's just so dumb," she said. "Somebody in our family's always had it. My father has it too, that's why he put the skylight in my attic, because he knows how I feel. I thought I was growing out of it. But just now it was really bad. I couldn't breathe." She grabbed her throat and pretended to choke.

"People kid you about it?"

"Never more than once." Her eyes narrowed. Then she widened them again. "But this time was the worst it's ever been. It was like the hedges were crowding in on me, eating up the sky bit by bit. And sucking away my air."

She took another deep breath and wilted against the bench.

Neil stood looking around glumly. "For me it was too easy."

"I feel so sorry for you!"

"I mean it. A maze is supposed to be a puzzle. But that last bit, with all the paths leading inward, that gave the whole game away."

There was no sign of the midnight wall-climber. Of course. Neil dropped his gym bag on the turf and asked himself what he'd expected to find. A jacket with a name tag?

"Besides," he said, "you can tell the Uglies have been here. The grass has been mowed. They must know the ins and outs of the whole maze. There's no mystery at all!"

"Maybe this isn't the real centre. The story goes, it's marked in a special way, with a natural spring."

"You know anybody who's actually seen this spring?"

"No . . . "

"So, maybe this fountain is it." That made him realize how thirsty he was. It had been dry and dusty between the yew walls. He stepped up to the stone column of the fountain and turned the tap on the side. Nothing came out of the nozzle except a smell of rust and mildew.

"And it doesn't even work!" He was disgusted. "This place is just as crumby as the house." He picked up his bag, still weighted down with marbles. Then he looked at Fleur. "Come on, let's get it over with. You can hold my hand if you want."

He wasn't teasing, but she flashed him a warning glance. She got up, looked at the gap in the hedge, and wet her lips.

They both stood still a moment, listening. Neil knew, now, why both the house and the maze made him so uncomfortable.

It was the utter quiet. It was so quiet, you kept straining your ears for the next sound. What that sound might be . . . A footstep, maybe. Somebody coming. Someone you wouldn't want to meet.

A sound did come. Music? It tinkled. Then Neil realized it was water flowing, very far away. A delicate, liquid sound that made his mouth feel parched.

"Where's it coming from?"

"The lake?" Fleur said doubtfully.

"No, it's *running* water. Maybe the pipes are broken under the ground, and that's why the fountain's dry."

It was too late to go looking for the hidden source, though. The yellow sky had faded to violet. Dark had come on quicker than Neil had expected. Now he was really mad at himself for making that mistake.

But it was still light enough to see the paths between the hedges. The white twine showed up clearly, and so did the marbles. He started picking them up while Fleur walked ahead of him, rewinding the twine. She kept darting glances around and overhead.

"You okay?" he asked.

"Yeah . . . no. I can breathe, but . . . " Her shoulders hunched.

Neil didn't tease her. He was jumpy too.

When the sounds began, he thought he was imagining them. Soft thuds like footsteps on damp ground, faint rustlings, even fainter breathing noises. He couldn't make out where they were coming from.

Fleur stopped. Her hands were wrapped so tightly around the roll of twine, her knuckles were whiter than the string.

"Somebody's in here with us," she whispered.

So it wasn't his imagination. Funny, how that wasn't much of a comfort.

"Probably just one of the Uglies." He pitched his voice loud. "Thinks he can chase us out of the maze! Well, he'll find out whose maze it is, pretty quick."

He held his breath. A moment later the sounds began again, a little louder. Now the rustling sounded like a large body creeping along on the other side of the hedge wall, low down.

"Let's get out of here," Fleur muttered.

Neil didn't really think it was one of the Uglies. It's the wall climber, he thought. Only now he's *creeping* after me. Crawling on the ground like an animal. This created a mental picture that raised goosebumps on his arms.

All the same . . . He began to walk back along the path, head bent, listening. Fleur grabbed his arm. "What are you doing?"

"He's in here somewhere. This time I'll get him. I'll make him answer questions."

"Neil, you're crazy! You . . . " Her hand locked onto his arm. "*Something's there.*"

"Where?" He whirled, searching the shadows.

"The hedge . . . is . . . moving . . . "

He followed the direction of her wide stare, and saw it. Above their heads, the foliage was stirring. One huge patch of it, about three feet across. As if a family of squirrels lived in there and had wakened up and begun stretching.

He started to say so. "Squ . . . " But no small animals chattered or ran out, and the patches of yew and the inky shadows were still moving in a strange silence.

They were taking the shape of an enormous mask.

The eyebrow ridge and nose were thin and straight, like an ancient helmet, but the wide, sad mouth curled down as if it were alive. Eyes seemed to look out at them from shadowy pits.

Neil backed up against Fleur. Sick fear and a growing wonder fought inside him. He would have run, except he'd recognized the face and couldn't take his eyes off it.

"I've been wrong," he said shakily. "It is Jasper I've been seeing. But it's not human. Not alive. It's a ghost."

Not ghost, not ghosss, hissed the wind in the hedge.

"I . . . I don't . . . under . . . " His lips went stiff.

The huge face loomed over him, sad and terrible. A breeze stirred the foliage, making the mouth move. *Not ghosssss . . .*

Fleur made no sound, but her nails dug into his arm.

"What . . . " he croaked. He swallowed and tried again. "What . . . are you?"

Jasssssss . . .

"Jasper? You're really Jasper?"

Yesss yesss oh yesss but hurryhurry, you musssssst run, runnn . . .
The voice was breathy and hoarse, like a rasp of twigs.

"But what are you? What's going on? How did you . . . "

Later later talk later, the yew twigs whispered. *Now get out get out, thingsssss, thingssss coming . . .*

"What things?" Neil couldn't look away from that horribly familiar face.

Bad thingssss . . . Dussssssk in maze . . . Time of changessss . . . Nevernever come in dussssk . . .

"But I've got to know . . . "

Getoutgetout! Getout! the wind shrieked suddenly. *Hurry-hurrry now! Hurrrrry . . .*

The wind fell silent. The hedge wall became a hodgepodge of shadows. Jasper's face was gone.

Neil stood shaking.

A moment later, low on the other side of the hedge, came a crashing and tearing of wood. As if something big was trying to claw through the tough stems to get at them.

Fleur yanked his arm, then she was flying. Neil left his bag where it lay and scrambled after her.

He threw himself along tunnels of darkness, guided only by a white thread at elbow height. He ran almost blind, till he began to think he was stuck in a nightmare, and the chase would never end.

Six

Neil burst from the maze into a clear blue twilight. The hillside fell away under his feet.

He pitched forward and rolled, letting gravity help him, not stopping till he splashed into the shallow stream at the bottom. Then he was up and running again, uphill toward the pines. Fleur was a blur of pale arms and legs on the slope ahead.

In the seconds it took to scramble to his feet, he'd glanced back. Clots of darkness were leaping down the hill after him.

"Fleur! The pines!" He had a crazy idea they'd be safe if only they could reach the top of the ridge, as if that was some kind of boundary.

Something breathed hoarsely behind him, a wet sound, hissing through teeth.

Two more strides, one more — something grazed his heel and screeched eagerly — then Neil took a frantic broad jump. He was at the top, springy boughs whipping his face.

Then his shoe caught in a loop of root and he crashed to the ground. He lay struggling for breath. A cold touch breezed along his back, over his head and past. His mind went dark.

When, minutes later, he realized he was still in one piece, he opened his eyes. Seeing only sprays of needles, sharp black against the dusk-blue sky, he sat up.

Fleur scrambled to her feet beside him. "What . . . " she began, then made a gulping noise.

Neither of them said anything as they slid downhill among the pines. Fleur stumbled between the lilacs and into the garden just in time to be caught in the beam of Gregory's headlights as he pulled up to the house.

Gregory drove Fleur home, with her bicycle sticking out of the trunk. Neil sat in the back seat.

"Up in the maze, eh?" Gregory glanced at Neil in the rear-view mirror. "Got it solved, have you?"

"Uh-huh. It was easy."

"Easy." Gregory gave Fleur a sharp sideways look. "Is that why the pair of you look like you've been dragged through a hedge backwards?"

Neil wondered why Fleur wasn't speaking up. She was usually pretty glib. But right now she sat like a stuffed doll, her eyes fixed straight ahead.

"Neil?"

"We . . . uh, fell a few times. It was dark. Don't worry, nobody got hurt."

"Well, don't push your luck. That maze is too near the bluff." Gregory's hands tightened on the wheel. "In fact, better stay away from there altogether after dark, okay? You could have a nasty fall."

Neil stared uneasily at the side of his father's face. It was almost an echo of the warning he'd been given in the maze. And yet it was just good sense. *He couldn't know, could he?*

Until they reached the Padgett house, Fleur huddled in silence. As soon as the car stopped, she was out and running up the front walk. While Gregory unloaded the bike, Neil chased Fleur and caught her at the door.

"We have to talk about it."

"Not now!" She had the door open and was halfway through it.

"Okay, tomorrow."

"Tomorrow I have to babysit Piglet." She was inside and facing him through a two-inch opening. Neil stuck his toe in the gap to hold it open.

"I wouldn't have thought you'd be such a wimp."

It was the right thing to say. A scowl wiped away the trace of panic in her eyes. "All right! Tomorrow. Two. After Piglet."

♋

Next afternoon about two o'clock Neil found her sitting on the front steps of the Padgett house, with a bowl of cheese puffs in her lap. She was watching her brother Richard, who was buried to the waist under the hood of his red Corvette. She waved orange fingers at Neil.

He wheeled his borrowed bicycle across the driveway and lowered the kickstand. Then he slumped onto the steps beside her, winded by the long push up Sentinel Hill.

"I like your house," he said.

Fleur glanced back at it and shrugged. It was a big, white, wooden house with a wide green verandah that needed to be scraped and repainted. Enormous silver maples arched over the front lawn. The only flowers were a border of fiery red geraniums.

"It's just ordinary. Not like yours."

"That's what I mean." He grinned.

"I'd rather live in yours any day." Her face lit up. "I've always wanted to climb that tower. Have you been up there yet?"

"Not yet." He wasn't sure why, but Dexter's house didn't invite exploring. Maybe with Fleur there it would feel less . . . well, unfriendly.

"About last night," he began.

Fleur cut him off. "I figured it out." Her cheeks reddened. "It was my phobia. It's never been that bad before, though. I guess that maze just got me so nervous, I started seeing things. Things that weren't there, I mean." She stuffed a handful of cheese puffs into her mouth.

Neil turned sideways to stare at her. "It had nothing to do with your phobia. I saw it too! It was my twin brother Jasper."

"Come *on*. You only saw it because I saw it first."

"But . . . "

Fleur wiped her fingers on her jeans, swallowed the last of the cheese puffs and jumped off the steps. She headed down the sidewalk, picking up her own bike from the lawn on the way.

Neil grabbed his bike and followed. He wasn't letting her go until he'd got this straightened out.

They walked their bicycles across the round park that crowned the hill top. Fleur detoured to take a drink from the fountain in the centre, near the children's sandbox, then put her thumb over the nozzle to make the water spurt up in a sparkling arc.

Neil dodged the falling drops. "I have to tell you about Jasper."

Fleur sighed heavily and turned her eyes skyward. "I have a feeling we're going to argue. But go ahead, talk."

It was a perfect summer day. Small kids shouted across the park, radio music sang from a window. Someone was cutting grass nearby, Neil could smell it.

On a day like this, the kind of story he had to tell was hard to swallow. But he tried to make Fleur believe. He talked quietly and calmly as they walked their bicycles down the curving streets to the centre of town.

He told her about Jasper, how he'd died as a baby along with their mother. How he used to imagine seeing his twin beside him, when all along he knew it was his own reflection.

"It was all pretend, till I came here, to Amstey. And then things started getting strange."

Seeing Jasper outside his second-floor window by night. Following him to the maze. Seeing him, next day, in the mirrored wall of the coffee shop.

"You saw your reflection again," Fleur called over her shoulder. The sidewalk was getting busier, so they had to go in single file.

"But he was trying to warn me about something, I saw his lips move. And then again, in the maze, that was him. And I didn't see any mirrors there!"

Fleur shook her head. "We were nervous. It's easy to imagine things when you're feeling edgy. Especially in the dark."

"This morning," Neil ploughed on, "I went back into the maze — after the sun was up, of course — to get the marbles and the string. They were gone. Nothing there. Not even a shred."

"The Uglies came and got them."

"So, nothing happened last night?" he yelled over the rumble of a passing farm truck. "What was chasing us, then?"

"Nothing was chasing us!" she yelled back. "Imagination!"

"Yeah? Well, take a look at this." Neil wheeled his bike over to a store window and propped it up. Fleur followed, curious. He unzipped the bag behind the seat, pulled out a wad of white cotton fabric and shook it out.

It was the T-shirt he'd been wearing yesterday. "I didn't see this till I took it off last night." He gave her a tight smile, then flipped the shirt to show the back.

The fabric was slashed into fluttering ribbons right up the middle.

"That's what I'd call a close shave," he said.

Fleur sucked on her lip. "Um . . . you caught it on a branch."

"Uh-huh."

"Look, Neil, I know what you're trying to tell me — but things like that just don't happen. In the movies, sure, but not in real life."

"Aren't you the one who was talking about magic yesterday? I see you're still wearing your good luck charm."

She waved her wrist, where the oval pendant glinted. "That's different! Everybody knows there's such a thing as luck. But you, with your Jasper and your monsters and all, that's just pretend."

Neil crammed the shirt back into the bag. The problem was, she was beginning to convince him.

What a letdown! He'd thought he was onto an idea. That Jasper was trying to tell him something, that it had to do with the maze, and that somebody else — or something else — was trying to scare him away from there.

Either way, it was obvious the maze held the answers. Or it had looked that way this morning. Now it looked like moonshine, and Neil felt he'd made a fool of himself.

"Forget it." Fleur grabbed her bike. "Let's go eat. Arguing always makes me hungry."

♋

Five minutes later Fleur, in the lead, whizzed around the corner of Simcoe onto Gunn Street and a quick two blocks east to the Amstey Market, where they left their bikes in a rack.

It wasn't a market day, so the ground floor of the old stone building was dim and deserted, and smelled of bleach and stale food. The counters were draped in white sheets.

"Up here." Fleur gripped Neil's wrist and pulled him up the wooden stairs to the second floor. "This is a great place. You can eat a dozen different kinds of food at once and watch everybody you know going past down there on the street."

"I'm not hungry."

"Well, I am."

They climbed out into the glow and chatter of an open area full of tables, with a wall of windows on one side and a row of fast food booths on the other. Greenish skylights opened the ceiling and tinted the sun that poured in over the people. Most of the tables were taken.

"There's one by the window. Get it!" Fleur gave Neil a push in the right direction. "I'll order the food."

A few minutes later she slipped into the chair opposite him. "Chicken nuggets and chips okay? They'll bring it when it's ready. You owe me $4.75."

Neil dug in his pocket and found most of the money, left over from what his father had given him yesterday. Then he looked around and caught his breath. "Again!"

"What?"

"Look over there. The stairs."

The stairwell was on the other side of the hall. Behind the railing was a head as round as a coconut under a peaked cap, turning this way and that. Two gloved hands grasped the railings. The hidden eyes swept across Neil's, then swung back and stopped moving. The back of Neil's neck went cold.

Fleur leaned from her chair. "I don't see . . . Oh."

"There, he's ducked down again. Fleur, he's trailing me. No doubt about it."

"That's silly! I mean, why shouldn't he come here? Uglies have to eat too!"

"Then why is he lurking in the stairwell? And, did you notice? He's still wearing those heavy gloves. Why? What's he hiding?"

"Maybe he has a terrible skin rash. You know, from those chemicals they use. Weed-killers and stuff."

"I guess that could be it." But he couldn't shake off that crawly feeling.

There was nothing behind the railing now, but Neil wasn't comfortable being in full view of the stairwell. He leaned forward, trying to keep a pillar between him and it. His elbow knocked over a plastic container. Sugar sprayed across the shiny black surface of the table.

He started brushing the grains into a heap. Then he saw what was under his nose and grew very still.

Fleur leaned over. "What is it?"

Between his hands, the tabletop showed black through the white sugar, in the shape of a letter H.

"It's Jasper," Neil whispered.

"You did that," Fleur said flatly.

"No. I barely touched . . . "

"Spare me!" She scuffed the spill with her hand. "You must think I'm an idiot!"

Neil caught her wrist. "Just look!"

His hands were nowhere near the sugar now, but another H had formed on the table. They both bent forward. A dark stroke ploughed through the white as they watched, then three short strokes jutted off from the longer one. An E.

Neil's face sank to six inches above the surface. From this close he could see it was not at all like a finger drawing lines in the sugar. It was more as if a tiny wind was blowing a furrow, scattering grains left and right.

Some of it suddenly sprayed at his mouth, as if someone had playfully flung a handful of sugar at him. He sat back, licking the sweetness from his lips and tingling with astonishment.

Fleur was still staring at the table, her eyes and mouth wide open.

A word had formed. H E L P. Then came a large curve, slow and wobbly. C.

"This is hard for him. You can see it." Neil's hands clenched on the edge of the table.

H . . . Still more slowly: A . . . Another long stroke . . .

Then a big, red-knuckled hand came from nowhere and swept across the table. The sugar was gone, and the message with it.

Seven

Can't you kids be more careful?" The waiter banged a loaded tray down on the table. "Don't ever think, do you?" His moustache lifted in a snarl.

Fleur's head went up. "As if we did it on purpose!" But the man was already yards away, barging between the tables. "What a jerk!"

Neil forgot him. Excitement bubbled through his veins as he helped Fleur unload the tray. Suddenly he laughed.

"Still think it's our imagination?"

She paused, pop can in hand. "Well . . . it's funny, but I kind of hope not." She looked embarrassed. "After all I said, too."

"Well, here's the proof. It just came to me. Remember that message on the window the first night? Think about it."

Her eyes went blank, then bright blue with surprise. "Of course! It gave my name, and Charlotte's. And you'd never heard of us before."

"Right. So that proves Jasper's real. And in trouble."

Fleur bit into a chicken nugget, then stopped with her mouth full. She gulped. "Oh, my holy . . . I've been talking to a ghost!"

"He's not a ghost. He said he wasn't."

"Then what is he?"

"We'll find out." Neil pushed his dishes to one side. He picked up the plastic container and shook a layer of sugar over the clear spot in the middle of the table. Then bent close to watch. He held his breath. *Come on, Jasper, come on . . .*

Sugar began to scatter. A dark point appeared and stretched to a groove. Letters formed slowly, a grain at a time. The effort was obvious. Neil clenched his teeth. H . . . E . . . L . . .

"Help Charlotte," Fleur said quickly. The sugar stilled. She glanced at Neil. "Think I'm right?"

He chewed his lip a moment, then bent close again. "Jasper. We'll try to make this easier. How about dots? I mean, one dot for yes, two dots for no. Okay?"

A spray of sugar, a sudden dark spot. Yes.

We're talking. Me and Jasper. Neil stared at the spot and his skin prickled all over. Tears pressed behind his eyes. He took a deep breath and forced himself to be logical.

"Charlotte was born — when? A hundred years ago?"

"More," Fleur said. "Gran said she vanished in 1849, and she was 18 then, so . . . "

"Well, come on. She has to be dead by now."

Two dots in the sugar, fierce and quick. No!

"You're sure you mean my Charlotte?" Fleur asked. "Charlotte Padgett?"

One dot for yes.

"But if she's alive, where is she?"

M . . . A . . .

"In the maze?"

One dot.

"But where in the maze?" Neil frowned. "We've been to the centre, it's empty. Where else is there?"

F . . . A . . . L . . . They had to wait, confused, as he spelled it all out. It seemed to take hours. Fleur mechanically finished all her chicken and fries as she watched, while Neil's grew cold.

FALSE CENTRE FIND TRUE.

"So there is another centre! That means . . . " Fleur's quick flare of triumph faded. "That means we'll have to go back in."

"I still don't get it, any of it." Neil studied the message, his head on his fists. "How can Charlotte still be alive? And where? And what's Jasper got to do with it?"

The grains were scattering again, letters labouring to form. H . . . E . . . "We know," Fleur said softly. "Help Charlotte. Neil, this is life and death to him. She must be in real trouble." She bent over the table. "Jasper, what kind of trouble is Charlotte in?"

A long pause. "He's gone," Neil said. Then the letters began straggling into shape. D . . . E . . . X . . . T . . .

"You two! Didn't I tell you?" The sour-faced waiter was standing over them, hands on hips. "I'm sick and tired of kids coming in here and vandalizing the place."

"Vandalizing!" Fleur was outraged.

Neil pushed back his chair. "Let's go. We'll find some place better."

♋

The stairwell was deserted. Neil kept a sharp eye out, but there wasn't an Ugly to be seen, inside the market or on the street.

They bought a box of salt at a corner store, then biked three blocks west to the war memorial. It stood in its own tiny park overlooking the lake, a triangle of grass with busy roads on two sides and an iron fence on the third. Two wide steps led up to a granite pedestal where a bronze soldier in a flat First World War helmet stood holding a rifle poised.

They were only interested in the steps, which were made of polished black marble. They sat down, spilled salt between them, and waited.

The black marble drank up the sunshine and grew hot and sweaty under them. Cars and trucks shot by, spewing gasoline fumes and dust. The breeze from the lake brought gulls screaming to be fed.

Half an hour later Neil scooped up the salt and hurled it into the air.

"That's not good for the grass," Fleur objected.

Neil growled and wiped sweat from his neck.

"This isn't the right kind of place. Too noisy." She looked around at the traffic. "Or he's still tired from last time. You could see it was getting harder and harder for him."

"Especially at the end. When he was trying to say . . . "

"Yeah, Dexter. Which doesn't make any sense."

She stuck the box of salt in her carrier basket. They pushed their bikes south along the boardwalk, cars whizzing by on the left, rocks and sand and hissing breakers to the right. The planks sent up a smell of warm creosote.

"Here's the story the way my gran tells it," Fleur said. "The Gunns — your bunch — were high-class people, and the Padgetts were . . . well, just ordinary storekeepers. Like we are now. But Dexter fell in love with Charlotte because she was the most beautiful girl around. And also the smartest."

She perked up her head and strutted beside her bike, acting the part. "He even built that tower just for her, did you know that? He added it on after the house was built. To be her special place, after they got married."

"So what went wrong?"

"Nobody knows. Maybe their families were against it because he was so much older. He was twice as old as she was."

"Or maybe she didn't like him."

"I don't see how that could be." She stopped acting and walked on, leaning on her handlebars. "He was incredibly handsome, and rich, and he'd been all over the world. All kinds of exciting places that nobody else had been. But then . . . " Her voice dropped to a whisper. "They vanished. Together. That kind of proves it, right?"

"Proves what?"

"Well, Charlotte must've really liked him, or she wouldn't have run off with him. I'll bet they eloped."

"And yet Jasper says . . ."

"Yeah, I know."

"I wish we could do more than just guess. We need to find out more about both of them. Fleur, where — "

"I know just the place!"

⚋

"Something about Dexter Gunn? Well . . . " Mr. Venables scratched thoughtfully among the few hairs on his head, then stabbed a finger at Neil and Fleur. "Follow me!"

He darted between two cliffs of towering antique wardrobes. Before they'd taken half a dozen steps after him they heard a creaking, crackling sound, then a yell.

Fleur was quickest off the mark. When Neil reached them he found the little man propping up a gigantic piece of furniture with his shoulder while he struggled to wedge a stack of books under one corner. A splintered wooden leg lay beside him.

Fleur had thrown all her weight against the thing. Neil added his, and for a moment it swayed backwards.

"Whoa!" Mr. Venables grabbed a door handle and the enormous bureau-desk-wardrobe — it looked like all three rolled into one — swayed forward again and crunched down on the stack of books.

"This thing is a menace!" Fleur let go cautiously, then eased a door open and peered into the deep hollow of the upper half. "Funny, it looks sort of familiar."

"This *thing*," Venables said gloomily, "is — or was — a fine example of a Victorian oak highboy. And it should be familiar, Fleur, it came from your house."

"My house?" She blinked at it. "Oh, yeah! When we cleared all that junk out of the attic to make room for me and Betts."

"Well, this isn't junk, not even with a broken leg. My fault, I'm afraid, for using it as a prop for old joints." Not touching the highboy, he lowered himself stiffly to his knees and started pulling books from the bottom of a set of shelves that stood nearby.

Neil knelt beside him. "Can we help?"

"You can take these." He loaded Neil's arms with dusty volumes. A dry, stale smell rose up. Neil sneezed.

Fleur picked up the topmost book and opened it as she led the way out from behind the wardrobes. "*Early Days in Amstey Township*," she read. Then her mouth opened wide. She pushed the book at Neil, her finger on a picture facing the title page.

He took one look and nearly lost his grip. Venables grabbed the stack of books from his arms and dumped them on the table.

"What? How . . . " The glossy paper was yellowed and stained, but you could see the man's face clearly. It was Neil's father, dressed up in dark, old-fashioned clothes. He stood framed in an onion-shaped archway.

"There he is!" Venables beamed at them. "The man himself."

"You mean . . . "

"Dexter Gunn. Fascinating likeness, isn't it?" Venables peered into Neil's face, then back at the picture.

Neil was barely listening to him. He was busy grasping the fact that the picture was a copy of a painting instead of a photograph, and the man was not his father.

Though Gregory had the same straight eyebrows and nose and wide mouth as Dexter, and the same dark hair and light eyes, the two faces were really very different. Dexter's eyes . . .

"Looks as if he could slay with a glance, doesn't he?" Venables said cheerfully, whacking dust off his trousers. "What's this in aid of, youngsters? Just filling an idle hour?"

"No, this is serious. Neil — " Fleur poked him in the side with her elbow. "Neil just found out about Dexter, and so of course he wants to know what he was like."

"Well, he won't find out much from these books." Venables thumped the stack and raised a puff of dust. "They're so painfully polite! You just know all sorts of nasty things were going on under the surface, but these histories never do more than tantalize."

"How do you know?" Neil closed the book but kept his finger in the place.

"You get snippets of the truth if you read between the lines. Do you know how Amstey was founded, Neil?"

Fleur broke in eagerly. "Oh, I know all that stuff, we took it in school. Dexter Gunn and John Amstey were partners. John got the settlers to come — including my family — and Dexter did the legal stuff and laying out the streets and all that."

"Right. And then the partners split up. You know why? Over a name. Dexter wanted the town named after himself."

Fleur laughed. "Dexterville?"

"No, Gunnville." Venables chuckled. "Doesn't sound much better, does it? It was the settlers who insisted on naming the town after Amstey. He was their first mayor, and a good one by all accounts. He edged out Dexter for the job. Then, a few years later, the two of them ran for parliament, and guess who won by a landslide?"

"John Amstey," Fleur chimed in.

"Exactly! And after that, the books say, Dexter retired to 'pursue his scholarly studies.'" Venables sniffed with amusement. "What they mean is, he went off in a huff. Sour grapes!"

"I wonder how come Charlotte liked him, then? Why would she elope with him?"

"If they did elope. I've often thought . . . " Then the door chimes tinkled and his head swung around. His eyes brightened. "Customer!" He headed for the front of the shop.

"I don't think he gets many," Fleur whispered.

Neil opened the book in his hand and took another look at the portrait. Those eyes . . . a shiver ran up his spine. He clapped the book closed and dropped it on top of the stack. "So long, Dexter. I'm glad you're not around!"

He almost wished they hadn't come. It was a letdown to discover this new-old relative, only to find out he was such a mean character.

Fleur had picked up another book and was flipping the stiff pages. Then she flattened it on the table. "Look, here's something I never saw before. It's a map of Amstey from the old days. Sure looks different from now, doesn't it?"

Neil bent over it, wrinkling his nose against the aged smell. The plan of the old town looked like a pair of snail shells lying side by side. The shell at the top was Sentinel Hill, with its streets curling down around the slopes.

"That's where I live." Fleur touched it. "And there's the downtown." She touched the centre of the snail shell at the bottom. Queen's Circle.

Something about the pattern nagged at Neil. "Why?" he wondered aloud. "Why didn't he just draw all the roads straight, the way they did in Toronto?"

Fleur sniffed. "Not every place has to be exactly like Toronto, in case you didn't know." She bent her head sideways to read the spines of the other books. "The rest of this stuff looks useless. Come on, I saw some pictures in that highboy."

When Neil caught up with her again she was visible only from the shoulders down, her head and arms deep inside the upper half of the massive cabinet. It was built like an earthmover and had to weigh hundreds of pounds, but as Fleur burrowed deeper it swayed again. Neil jumped forward to brace himself against it.

"There's all kinds of neat stuff in here!" Her voice sounded miles away. "Old photos, and some beads, and newspapers, and . . . "

"And spiders." One was crawling on her shoulder.

Fleur froze, then flung herself back out of the cabinet. It rocked backward, then forward again onto the stack of books. They shifted, slid . . .

Neil had the oddest feeling that it was all happening in slow motion. He could see Fleur making a dive to the left, he could see himself leaping in the opposite direction. Their two bodies arced away as the highboy toppled between them.

Then came a crash, and the floorboards bounced, and small glass and metal objects tinkled all over the shop. The air was thick with dust.

"Fleur! Neil! What happened?" Venables was there, tripping over scattered bits of drawers, before they had time to pick themselves up.

Fleur was red with embarrassment. Ignoring the dirt smudges all over her jeans and T-shirt, she started picking up sheaves of crackling newspapers and scraps of ribbon, as if that would help put the wreck back together.

Neil worked his fingers under the highboy's frame, thinking to push it upright, but Venables waved him back. "Leave it alone. You'll only pull more of it loose."

"I guess we owe you."

"Well . . . maybe it can be rebuilt. Maybe." Venables crunched away, shaking his head. Neil looked after him guiltily.

"Guess we better go before we trash the place." He headed for the door. Realizing Fleur wasn't with him he stopped and looked back. She was staring down at an armful of torn papers, with a scrap of ribbon dangling from it.

"Neil, wait. This is . . . this could be . . . "

"Come on, let's just get out!" He pulled the door open with a clatter of chimes and stepped out onto Simcoe Street.

It was close to supper time, he judged by the emptiness in his stomach. The sun was hot on his back. The breeze was off the lake and smelled weedy and fishy, but it was fresh compared to the stale air in the antique shop.

He picked up his bike from the lane beside the shop and pushed it slowly along the street. Fleur caught up with him at a little stone bridge that crossed the creek. The slope of Sentinel Hill rose ahead.

"I'm wondering," he said. "If I get my dad to lend me the money, how long would it take me to pay it back?"

"Money for what?"

"The highboy. We can't just leave it like that."

"We? That was my fault. I'll work it out with my parents."

But she spoke as if all but the tip of her mind was submerged in something else. He saw she still had the papers she'd salvaged from the highboy, piled in her carrier basket. Some of them looked like old magazines.

"What've you got there?" He propped his bike against the parapet and reached into her basket. "*Popular Science*, November, 1921 . . . *Saturday Night*, May 3, 1919 . . . *Scribner's* . . . Hey, these could be worth something. They should go back to Mr. Venables."

"Oh, I'll take them back. Later." There was an odd quiver in her voice. "You'll never guess what I found."

At first he didn't realize what he was seeing when she pushed the paper under his nose. Faded handwriting slanted neatly across the brown-spotted pages. *My dear Walter*, it said. *It has been some weeks since I . . .*

"The date." Fleur's finger tapped the page. "The date!"

"February 18, 1849," he read aloud. Then it hit him. "Fleur, this is really old. It could be valuable!"

"It is to me, anyway. Look who signed it!" She flipped the page. *Your loving sister, Charlotte.* "And that's just the first one. There's a whole bunch here!"

"I suppose it could be some other Charlotte . . . "

"No way!" Her voice quivered with excitement. "These are my Charlotte's letters, written the same year she disappeared. Neil, we could have the answer to the mystery right here!"

Eight

This will drive me crazy," Neil said.

After exploding her bomb, Fleur calmly folded up the letter and slipped it, along with the others, inside one of the old magazines. At least, she pretended to be calm. The magazine fluttered in her hands.

"The letters will have to wait. If I'm late for dinner I'll be skinned." She wheeled her bike onto the side of the road, straddled the crossbar and pushed off.

He laboured up the hill after her. "But that means . . . I won't know anything . . . until tomorrow!"

"Sure you will. You'll eat with us."

"But your parents!"

"We have extra people all the time. No big deal!"

♋

"Fleur's house!" Neil shouted into the phone. "No, Fleur. For dinner!" He held one hand over his free ear. All the Padgetts were home, and more than half of them were in the living room with him, talking over his head.

"Oh, Fleur." Gregory chuckled softly, Neil wasn't sure why. "I met some old school friends and I was going to have you eat out with us, but never mind. Still . . . how will you get home?"

"I'll be fine. I'll bike."

"Make it before sunset, okay?"

"Don't *worry*, Dad."

But dinner took longer than he would have thought possible. The Padgetts took their food seriously. There was a lot of it, all delicious, much of it hot in spite of the weather — steaming platters of roast beef, bowls of cheese-covered potatoes, baskets of warm rolls that kept getting filled up again.

Fleur's Gran kept sending more food along the table to him, and he was soon full to bursting. Everybody else kept eating, yet none of them stopped talking for longer than half a minute.

At first Neil felt warm and happy as the talk and laughter bubbled around him. After an hour of it he felt his head was straining to explode.

"You're spared from dishwashing tonight, Fleur." Her father leaned back and winked at her. She reddened, leaped from her chair and poked Neil's shoulder in passing.

"Thanks . . . " He looked from Fleur's father to her mother to her grandmother. They'd all cooked. "Um, everyone. It was great."

He followed Fleur out onto the front porch and closed the door. For a moment he stood still, enjoying the quiet. The sun sat low in the trees, but there was plenty of light to read by.

Fleur was perched on the top step, busy unfolding the letters and making a flat sheaf of them. Neil flopped down beside her and put a hand on his stomach.

"I'm surprised I can walk!"

"Mm? You didn't eat that much. Gran will wonder why you were picking at your food." She was already bent over the first letter. "Oh . . . so that's why she was writing to her brother."

"Why? Was she away somewhere?"

"No, he was. He'd be my umpteen-great-grandfather, I guess. This first one talks about how she wishes she were with him in Toronto. Amstey must've been a quiet place in 1849."

"Like it's not now?" He hurried on, before Fleur could snap. "And Dexter'd been everywhere and seen everything."

"Yeah, listen." She held up the yellowed sheet to catch the light that slid along the verandah. "'He has seen the Horn of Istanbul, and the Rock of Gibraltar, and smelled the Cedars of Lebanon. He has visited holy men in Arab lands, and taken coffee with Turkish princes, and studied in the libraries of Egyptian pashas. If only I could have been there!' What's a pasha?"

Neil leaned back against the verandah pillar. "Don't know. But it's easy to see why Charlotte thought he was so wonderful. She wanted to see all those places too, but she was only a girl."

Fleur made a face. "That wouldn't have stopped me!"

"Well, maybe in those days it would have."

"No way!" She slipped the first letter to the back. "This next one . . . " She frowned over it. "There's some blotches, it's hard to read. Something about how she'd thought it would be so romantic to live high up in a tower."

Neil sniffed.

"Well, it would! But then Dexter actually had a tower built for her. Imagine how that would floor you!"

"Why would he do that?" He peered over her shoulder, but she pushed him off and held the page away.

"She says: 'At first I thought he was joking; but then, he never jokes. I fear it is true, that he has taken some fancy of mine in earnest. And it can only mean one thing, that he intends to ask to marry me.'" She laid down the page. "And then she says she'll say no. Now, why wouldn't she marry him? You can tell he's the best thing in sight."

"Maybe there was somebody else."

"I don't think so. This next one is all about a trip she's planning, but I can't read half of it, it's all blotched."

"Let me." He grabbed it from her hand and held it up to the light, while Fleur frowned over the next one. "So that's it," he said at last. "She was working on her father to let her go to Europe, to see Granada and Crete and Egypt, and all those other places Dexter'd told her about."

Fleur stretched and smiled. "Well, of course! It wasn't enough for her to sit and listen. She had to go and do it herself!"

"What happened next?" Neil was getting wrapped up in this.

"Mm. This one's really hard to read. Looks like she wrote it in a hurry." She showed it to him. Charlotte's neat, flowing script had become a scrawl.

"'He has asked me to marry him,' she writes. And she says no, and then . . . " Fleur held the sheet closer to her eyes. "Seems like everybody's mad at her. Her mother and father can't understand why she'd turn the man down, rich and a good name and all that. And of course the trip to Europe's off."

"That stinks! Well, and then what?"

She picked up another page only half filled with writing.

"Let's see . . . 'Today he has sent asking me to meet him. I have decided to go, if only to make him understand once and for all that I have no mind to marry anyone, not for years yet.' Then there's a bit I can't read, and then: 'Surely he, who has seen and done so much, will understand why I cannot set down my roots here in Amstey.'"

She looked at the next page and shuffled the stack together.

"Well? Don't stop there! Where's the next letter?"

"There is no next letter." She slapped the thin sheaf of papers against her knees. "That's the last one."

"That's it? So what do we know, after all that?" Neil pushed himself off the steps and stared glumly along the street.

"We know they met at least one more time."

"Yes, but then what?"

"One thing I know." Fleur was suddenly fierce. "She wasn't planning to run off with Dexter. Or anybody. She was all set to take off on her own."

"It sounds like that, doesn't it?" He picked up his bike from beside the steps and gave the handlebars a shake. "But where did they go? Did he push her into the lake and jump in after?"

"No, Jasper says . . . "

"Yeah, in the maze. And alive. So I'll just have to go back there. Though what use it'll be . . . "

"When do you want me to be there?" She was folding up the letters, but her hands were not as steady as her voice.

"You?" He stared. "You don't have to come. You'll hate it."

"Yes, I do have to come. I'll bet Charlotte wouldn't've let that place scare her. Just promise not to go without me!"

"Okay, we'll go tomorrow morning. It'll be different in daylight. I'll show you the tower first."

Fleur yelped with delight and leaped off the steps. For a moment he was afraid she was going to give him a hug right there on the front walk, in full view of the street. Then she looked at his face, laughed and stepped back.

"Remember." She pointed sternly. "No exploring without me!"

After she went inside, Neil straddled his bicycle and took a moment to wonder what it must be like to be a part of that family. Always with someone breathing down your neck. Never private, never quiet. Never lonely, either.

All the windows in the house were open, and voices drifted out, though he couldn't make out the words. Someone — it sounded like Fleur's father — laughed, and others joined in.

Standing alone in the dark, listening, Neil felt small and cold. He had often felt alone, but never as lonely as this.

Swiftly he rose on the pedals and swooped away into the darkness under the overhanging trees. He pushed the loneliness firmly into a back corner of his mind. He had other things to think about.

He hadn't wanted to mention to Fleur that he thought they were being followed again on the way home from Venables' antique shop. If she was afraid of looking like a wimp, so was he. Coincidence, she'd say. Maybe it was.

But as he cycled out of Amstey along Highway 21, he started to feel it again, that prickling between the shoulder blades that makes you want to turn and look back.

Yet nobody was following him. Headlights filled his rearview mirror, then flashed past him on the road. Then another set, then another.

It was only as he stopped on a long, tough slope and began pushing the bike that he looked back and saw it. In the stream of cars leaving Amstey, it was the snail. So slow that all the other traffic was passing it with impatient honks. By the silhouette, it was a pickup truck.

Just a slow one, Neil told himself.

As slow as a bike, came the dry reply from the back of his mind. As slow, right now, as a bike being walked.

He ran the bike up to the crest, hopped on and arrowed down the other side. Cars flashed past, and then a pickup. His glance caught a man's face fixed on the road, ignoring him: then gone. Neil relaxed. So that was that.

More cars passed, a van, a truck, with spaces of quiet and darkness between them. The stream of outbound traffic was drying up. Good, Neil thought, as he toiled up another hill and started on the long, lovely downward swoop.

A tractor-trailer loomed up over the hill and was down on him like a landslide, lights blinding, horn blasting. Its blizzard of dust caught him and tried to fling him off the road.

He braked, scattering gravel, and stood there rubbing grit from his eyes while the monster wheels roared past. The next bend swallowed the uproar.

Little by little, the night grew quiet. A nighthawk cried overhead, tracing its invisible circles. Crickets chirped. Neil found his night eyes, and the dark world opened out to him, the land whitening under the rising moon. He was alone on the road.

Alone for half a minute. Then the crest behind him was black against a sudden glow. The glow brightened to a dazzle as the headlights eased up and over. A pickup truck, creeping along like — he couldn't help thinking it — like a cat after a bird.

He pushed off. In seconds he was up to top speed, his knees burning. His rearview mirror caught the lights still far behind. The truck had speeded up slightly. It was pacing him.

He couldn't be far from home now. Home! That was a joke. But at least it meant safety. He hoped. And cars were still travelling the road, or bound to come along. No need to panic. He bent over the handlebars and pumped like a piston engine.

For a few minutes he thought he was going to make it. Then the bike rose to another crest and he grabbed a swift glance back, then forward. By moonglow he could see for miles in each direction and all he saw was a black ribbon of highway, empty except for himself and the pickup.

On both sides, the vague darkness of trees. Off to the east a few farm lights gleamed, but they were distant and faint.

The pickup was close behind him, and getting closer. If they wanted him, this was the time. Nobody else would see. His sweaty hands slipped on the rubber grips.

A panicky voice inside yelled at him to ditch the bike, head for the trees, hide! But he knew his only chance of safety lay on the road, where the next minute might bring another car. Or not.

The lights behind crept nearer. Gaining on him, but slowly. Maybe it was innocent, after all. Maybe it was a case of engine trouble, faulty brakes, a nervous driver . . .

The engine roared. The headlights brightened eagerly, flinging his shadow down the road. Neil poised over the seat, straining for more speed. The slim wheels were already whistling on the pavement, almost lifting off.

Then a gust of hot breath rolled over him, and the dazzle of light was all around him. One glance back: a metal snout was nuzzling his rear fender. And then the bike did lift off, and he was flying, light and darkness whizzing around him like a great wheel.

♋

He was dazed and bruised, but not in much pain. *I was lucky,* he thought vaguely, but he couldn't get a clear view of things. People moved around him, metal scraped pavement — that was his bike being picked up — then hands pressed up under his elbows and he was on his feet, swaying. The biting sourness in his mouth told him he had been sick.

Still too dazed to see properly, he climbed. Then he felt himself shut inside a small space that smelled strange. A smooth, cool surface under his hands proved soft when he pushed at it. Padded vinyl. *I'm in that truck.* His mind shook clear and his eyes focused.

He was wedged into the cab of the pickup truck, between the two Ugly Brothers. The truck was moving. It was too late to make a dive for the door, even if he could have reached it. He pulled his elbows tight against his sides and tried not to shiver. The odd smell was stronger now.

"You arre not hurrt."

After a moment, Neil guessed the driver had spoken. It was hard to tell: the dashboard lights barely picked out the face to his left, and the trap-like mouth had hardly moved. The voice was peculiar, a gravelly rumble, as if it had to squeeze up through a drainpipe instead of a throat.

"Not hurrrt, boy." It sounded like an order but was meant as a question, he realized.

"N-no. But the bike . . . " It was all he could manage. He wished they wouldn't press so close.

The smell: he knew now. It was them. It made him think of dogs, only more bitter.

"In back."

Twisting his head, he took a look out the rear window into the box and found himself gaping into a trio of faces, a row of them squashed together, staring in at him. All alike, all blank, except for the glinting slivers of eyes.

He faced front and hunched. "Wha . . . " He choked.

"Home. Safe."

"Sstay ssafe, boy." That was the one to his right. A higher voice, reedy and rasping, as if he had a bad cigarette habit. Only he didn't smell of tobacco smoke, just . . . what was it?

"Play in sssun. Sstay out of maze."

"Stay away from old books and old darrk trrrees."

Neil's eyes told him the truck had turned into his own side road. Only his eyes were working normally. His body was cold and limp and sore. His mind was in panic, throwing itself against its bone walls like a rabbit in a trap.

Their smell filled his mouth with a bitter dryness. He still didn't know what it was. He only knew what it wasn't. It wasn't human.

The truck pulled up in front of the house. A bumping noise came from the box. The two Uglies in the cab stayed put, still trapping Neil between them.

"Look, boy," rumbled the driver.

Neil looked. He had no choice. The driver turned his head and opened his eyes wide. It was like watching shades going up behind stained glass windows.

Yellow eyes, glowing with a hungry light. With black vertical slits of pupils, like a cat's.

The trap of the mouth cracked and the tips of white spikes glistened. "Be warrned."

From the right, a gloved hand gripped his arm. "Sstop thinking questionsss." The hand tightened. Through the fabric of the finger ends, sharp points pierced through. They dug into Neil's skin like curved needles. He stopped breathing.

Now he knew why they always wore those gloves.

Nine

Neil didn't see or hear much else until he found himself alone on the driveway in front of the house, kneeling beside the sprawled bicycle. He felt numb.

After a few minutes he stopped running his hands over the spokes — no damage was done — and found his way into the house by the door in the base of the tower.

There were no lights on, his father wasn't home. When the door closed behind him he might have stepped inside a cave under a mountain, it was that dark. And there were noises coming from what sounded like miles away. Faint creakings, whispers . . .

Something fluttered cool on his cheek and he yelled. In ten seconds he was in the kitchen, with the light blazing down. He leaned against the counter and shivered.

"Why'm I so cold? Those faces . . . "

Those three faces, each a copy of the others, in the pickup window. All squashed together so they could get a good, close look at him. They looked like . . .

"But there couldn't be *five* Uglies all alike! I must've been dreaming! When I fell off the bike it must have knocked me silly." He scrubbed his hands through his hair, and found a sore spot. But it didn't feel bad enough to have caused visions.

He went to stand by the window. Outside was blackness. Then he realized how exposed he was. Anyone could look in through the window, while he was as good as blind.

In sudden panic he leaped at the light switch and slapped it off again. Then he groped back to the door at the base of the tower. *I'm not staying in here alone. It's like . . .*

For a moment the words escaped him. Then a picture came. A gigantic animal crouching in the dark, and between its paws a tiny shivering mouse.

He wrestled the door open and stumbled out into the moonlight. Here, at least, he didn't feel trapped.

Then he tensed. Something droned in the distance, grew louder, nearer . . . an engine. *They're coming back.*

Blades of gold swept across the grass, then the motor died and the light too. A car door slammed. A car, not a pickup. The numbness began to fade.

Quick steps on the brick walk, a black shape suddenly right in front of him. He threw himself at it.

"Hey, what's this? Neil? What's the matter?"

Neil made himself let go and step back. His cheeks were hot. "Nothing." He led the way back into the house.

"Why are all the lights out?" Gregory snapped a switch by the stairs, then grabbed Neil's shoulder and swung him around. "Good grief! What happened?"

Neil flinched under his grip. His left shoulder ached, where it hit the ground after his fall from the bike. "I, uh . . . had a small accident. My bike skidded."

He looked down at himself. Another T-shirt filthy, his second-best pair of black jeans ripped on the knee. He wondered why he wasn't spilling the story of the Uglies.

"How did you get this?" Gregory took him by the wrist and held up his right arm. Four red marks, four spots of dried blood showed on the upper side. A matching nick showed underneath.

Neil's stomach knotted. So that part had been real, anyway. And he thought: tell him. Tell him everything.

He met Gregory's worried eyes and opened his mouth, and then he closed it again. Sure, tell him about Jasper sending you messages in sugar. And he'll sit you down and talk about when you were little, and you used to imagine Jasper being there.

"I fell. That's all."

Gregory let go of his arm. He knew there was more to it. He crossed to the sink, ran water into a kettle and set it on the stove. As he opened the cupboard, found cups and tea bags, he talked without looking at Neil.

"The place is getting to you, isn't it? Me, too. Well, we won't have to put up with it much longer. I think we may possibly have a buyer. He's coming out tomorrow to look the place over."

Neil laughed. "Who would want to buy this dump?"

"It's not a dump — just big and rickety. The man's looking for an unusual building to make into a hotel. Of course," he added casually, his eyes on the kettle, "you don't have to stay if you're bored. You can leave tomorrow, if you like."

Send me away from Jasper? "No! No, I want to stay."

A silence, while Gregory turned and studied his face. "Are you sure? You could stay with your Aunt Nan."

"I'm not bored," Neil said carefully. "I've got a friend."

"Fleur Padgett." Gregory smiled, and for some reason Neil felt embarrassed. "Well, if you're sure."

"I'm sure, Dad."

Neil reran the conversation in his head as he washed up in the bathroom. It gave him an odd, heavy feeling, as if he'd done something wrong.

But *it's not as if I was lying, really*, he told himself. *I just couldn't tell him. He wouldn't believe. Maybe I wouldn't believe it myself, except . . .*

Except the evidence was printed in dark bruises all over his left shoulder and arm. But he hardly looked at them. It

was his right forearm that made him feel sick, where the
marks of five sharp nails had dug in.

Stay away from the maze. Stop thinking questions. It would
be smart to do as they said.

He scrubbed the arm hard. The marks stung, but he felt
better once he was sure they were clean.

♋

When he woke next morning he lay in a comfortable haze,
aware something ugly skulked just beyond the edge of sleep,
but determined not to know about it. He lay on his back
among tangled sheets, staring up at the cracked ceiling.

He had never looked at it properly before. The light was
a stained-glass box, with green ivy shapes curling over an
amber background. It hung by a chain from a plaster medallion in the middle of the ceiling.

The medallion was a decorated circle three feet across, full
of narrow shapes like a nest of snakes twining around and
trying to bite each others' tails.

Snakes? Neil stared upward.

Sheets flew as he shot out of bed.

Not snakes. Hedges!

♋

He was sitting on the edge of a stone urn in front of the house
when a bicycle bell tinkled in the distance. A minute later
Fleur came streaking around the bend in the drive, scattering
gravel.

She leaped from her bike and let it crash to the ground.

"I got here as soon as I could! What *is* it?"

"You didn't have to rush. I've been looking around, and
maybe my idea wasn't so hot after all."

"Looking around? But you promised not to explore the maze without me!"

"Not the maze. The house. C'mon, I'll show you."

He got up and led the way to the open front door. The stucco house was glowing an angelic white in the morning sunshine. He watched the way Fleur looked up at it, bright-eyed and admiring.

Then grinned when she got a close look at the iron knocker. It was shaped like a dog's head, with the ring gripped in snarling jaws.

Fleur shaped a silent whistle. "Wow, this is eerie. What a twisted mind somebody . . . "

Her voice died as she crossed the threshold, and the heavy door swung closed behind her. They stood in a lobby like a church, a dim and echoing space that rose to a sky-blue ceiling two storeys above.

"Oh . . . " Fleur breathed. "This is miles better than I even imagined. This is . . . it's like being in another world."

She walked carefully out across the mosaic pavement. Bands of colour glowed under their sneakers. Emerald vines twisted among gilt leaves and ruby flowers.

"See the animals?" Neil pointed at the floor, and Fleur bent to look. You could just spot them slinking among the vines: thin sinewy hounds and spotted cats.

"This is gorgeous!"

"It's a maze, too," Neil said. He traced a snaky vine with his toe. "And over here." He crossed to the wall, which was covered with glossy tiles to shoulder height. Stars, diamonds, squares, in dark reds and blues, separated by twisting grooves of white plaster.

Fleur rubbed her hands up her folded arms. "It's cold in here. You wouldn't think it was August."

She was looking around doubtfully now. With her eyes used to the dimness, Neil knew, the lobby looked less wonderful.

Bits of stone were missing from the mosaic and many of the wall tiles were cracked.

The only piece of furniture was a bulging umbrella stand made of leather, with one broken black umbrella in it. The stand looked as if it might have been part of some large animal's leg a hundred years ago. A rhinoceros or an elephant, maybe.

Neil led the way through a doorway to the left, between two halves of an iron lattice gate. "Another maze," Fleur said, as she touched the iron curls.

Beyond the gate was a series of cool, dark rooms, all leading into each other and facing onto the courtyard. Tall slits of windows hid behind velvet drapes that were like spills of dark blue and purple ink.

Wherever you looked, patterns formed in the dimness.

Twining vines on the tiled walls. On the ceilings, plaster medallions full of gilt knotwork, circling the hanging lights. Floors of inlaid wood in interlocking stars, carpets that were a jungle of curls and twists.

"Mazes everywhere!" Fleur shook her head in wonder.

"Yeah, and I thought I'd found the answer. I thought I'd found a map of the maze." He told her about the pattern around the light over his bed. "But there's not enough of it." He waved a hand at the carpet, the walls, the ceiling. "None of these bits makes a complete maze."

"D'you think maybe old Dexter was dropping hints?"

"I think he wanted people to think so," Neil said sourly.

"Well, suppose we collected all the bits we could find, copied them onto paper — then fit them together! Like a big jigsaw puzzle." Fleur threw out her hands and beamed.

Neil sniffed. "That would take months! And ten to one it wouldn't be the right pattern when you finished. No, this whole house is one big practical joke."

He jerked his chin at a picture on the wall. In the dimness, she hadn't noticed it. "There he is. Grinning his head off at us idiots running around after clues!"

"You talk as if he's still here!" Fleur laughed. Then Neil turned on a lamp, so she could get a good look. Her smile died.

It was the original of the picture in Mr. Venables' book. Here, you could see a lot more detail. Dexter stood in an onion-shaped arch, against a distant view of misty blue hills.

Against the pale background he was a dark pillar. The only light touches were his face, the edges of white linen at his wrists and neck, and an oval shape on a gold chain looped across his black waistcoat. The wide, thin mouth was grave. The eyes smiled, but they were ice.

"He's laughing inside," Fleur said. "Only I don't think I'd like the joke. It's probably about me."

Then she stepped closer and peered hard. "Oh," she said flatly. For a moment she stood still, one hand circling the other wrist. Then she pulled off her chain bracelet and held it out to Neil, the pendant dangling. He stared at it, puzzled.

"Yours," she said. "Or maybe your father's."

"Did I miss something?" He didn't touch it.

"If you look in that painting, you'll see it on Dexter's watch chain. Remember I told you I found it?"

"Well?"

"It was on the beach, near here. Down below the maze, in fact. Stuck between two big rocks, just under the water."

"That must be the place where they met, the last time!"

"Right," Fleur said darkly. "The place where he grabbed her. Can't you just see it? She must've fought back. And the pendant got torn off, and he didn't notice."

"Or didn't care. It may not be worth anything."

"Well, it must be worth something now. It's old. Take it!"

He took the pendant between his fingers, enjoying its silky smoothness. No wonder Fleur liked it so much. He moved it to and fro, and the curled threads in the milky depths gleamed, and seemed to move.

"Neil. Inside . . . " Fleur was breathing on his hand. "Look, I never noticed before . . . "

For a moment he blazed with excitement. Then he shook his head. "This can't have anything to do with the maze. There's a sort of pattern in there, but you can't really see it."

He dropped the bracelet back into her hand. "Anyway, finders keepers."

☞

Neil led the way out into a stone-floored space behind the dining room. A yellow-grey brick staircase curled up around a thick pillar of brick.

"The tower." He waved. "You first."

Fleur stepped forward eagerly and started up. "I'd love to have my bedroom in a tower, wouldn't you?" she called over her shoulder. "It's why I moved into the attic with Betts. I like being up high in the sky. There's so much more space!"

"Great exercise too," Neil puffed.

The stairs seemed to wind upward forever, mostly in the dark. Fleur grew quiet.

The brick steps flaked and gritted under their shoes. When Fleur touched the outer wall, a painted tile dropped off and went crashing downward.

"Oh, no! I'm sorry."

"Not your fault. It's the place, it's falling apart."

She took the last four steps at a run, and Neil was right on her heels. The room above was bright, after the dark stairwell. They walked out into the middle of the veined pink marble floor and Fleur turned in a circle, to get the full effect.

Neil could tell she was all set to be delighted. But . . .

"Where are the windows?" she demanded.

When you stood in the garden looking up, the top of the tower seemed to be ringed all around with tall, slender arched windows. You expected to find a room full of light. From here, though, you could see most of the arches were filled in with plaster behind the lattices. Only two actually let you look out.

Neil went to the nearest. "Look, you can see the maze. Just the outside hedge, though. You can't see in."

"Do they open?" Fleur sounded casual. Too casual. He wrenched at the catch of the window.

"I think it's rusted shut."

"Never mind." She took a deep breath, then wrinkled her nose. "What's that smell?"

Neil looked around. Half the tiles had fallen off the walls, and in the plaster behind, big green-black patches spread like the scum on a lake.

"Mildew," Fleur said. "The place is rotting away."

"I guess they never bothered heating the tower. A hundred and fifty winters can do a lot of damage."

She nodded, and took another deep breath.

"Let's get out. It's bothering you." He touched her arm.

She shook him off irritably. "I'm okay! There's lots of air in here, good air. See how high the ceiling is?"

They both looked up and Neil caught his breath. The walls rose to a high, domed roof. A dark blue vault, a scoop of midnight, glinting with silver stars. For a moment he forgot his growing dislike of the place.

Then a section of plaster cracked away from the dome and fell, its stars still glinting, till it shattered into pieces at their feet. Spiders ran from it in all directions.

Fleur jumped back with a shriek, slamming against the wall.

"Scared of spiders?" Neil was ready to tease, but she wasn't looking at him. She was glaring past him with eyes that grew bigger and bigger until the blue irises were rimmed all around with white. Smudges of dust stood out on her ghost-pale face.

He looked around quickly, but nothing was there to stare at. Nothing he could see, anyway. A river of cold ran down his spine.

"What are you looking at? What's wrong?"

She didn't seem to hear. He shook her by the arm. She didn't notice, didn't move. She stood rigid, with her bent elbows tight to her sides and her hands spread out in front.

"Fleur!"

He gripped her shoulders and shook hard. Suddenly she shuddered and looked at him. Her eyes were wild and blank, hair over her face, barrettes scattering.

She stared at him as if she didn't know him, then pushed him away and was off down the stairs in a shower of broken brick.

Ten

"Neil, it happened. I'm not kidding. I was in some other place." Fleur kicked a pebble through an incoming wave.

Neil was still sceptical. He'd followed her as she ran down the stairs, out the door and straight to the gate in the back fence.

The gate opened onto a flight of log steps set in the bluff, down to a strip of sand and pebbles, and the lake. Fleur flew down the stairs so fast, he was afraid she'd break her neck.

Once on the beach, she spent five minutes just breathing. Then she talked.

It was the spiders that shook her, first of all. "*Not* that I'm scared of bugs. It was seeing them run out like that, all of a sudden."

And then she'd stepped back and the wall was there, much closer than she'd remembered. As if it had moved. As if it was shrinking in around her. Then her head spun, and the floor twisted out from under her feet and sucked her down into the dark.

"I was somewhere else. There was no mildew smell. And I was sitting on something soft."

"You were standing," Neil objected.

"I was sitting. On velvet, I think." Her fingers smoothed the air. "You know how velvet lies down one way and ruffles up the other? It was like that. Really deep and thick."

She took another deep breath. "Or it might have been a cat's fur."

"But if you were sitting on it . . . " Neil grinned.

"I know. It couldn't have been a cat. It had to be a big armchair, one of those old-fashioned kind that goes up behind your head and reaches out wide on the sides. But, Neil . . . " She gulped. *"That chair wrapped its arms around me."*

The sun beat down, but he felt cold. "You had a nightmare."

"I wasn't asleep. And it was too real. I could feel the bones under the velvet, like you can when you're holding a cat."

"You're sure it wasn't just the old phobia?"

"The old phobia never did that to me!" She knelt to scoop a chunk of sparkling stone out of the water. "I think, just for a second, I was where Charlotte is. And it was horrible!"

She tossed the stone away and shot to her feet. "Neil, we've got to find her!"

"We'll find her, all right." He wished he was sure. "Look, there's things you have to know before you get in any deeper. Like about the Uglies."

He told her about last night's ride home, as they scrambled along the beach. When he came to the part where he'd felt the claws through the gloves, she shuddered.

"Stop thinking questions." Her shoulders hunched. "I don't like the sound of that. Does it mean they can read our minds?"

"I don't know. What it means is, this is worse than we thought. I wouldn't blame you if you backed out now."

"Why?" She narrowed her eyes at him. "Are you backing out?"

"No."

"Why not?"

He shrugged, and stooped for a stone. "I hate to let a puzzle get the better of me."

"That isn't all. There's Jasper too." She poked his bruised arm. "Right?"

"Ow! Right, but you don't have to . . . " He tried skipping the stone. It sank at once.

"For me there's Charlotte. After reading her letters, I feel like I've always known her. Like she's my big sister. And there's Jasper, too. He's Charlotte's friend, so he must be okay. Anyway, Neil, you're stuck with me."

♋

"I still don't know what the Uglies are," Neil said as they walked back to the house to collect his supplies. "But one thing's sure. They want to keep us out of the maze so bad, we know that's where the answer's got to be."

Fleur insisted on coming too, so long as they were out before dusk. She kept her mind on the job of paying out string, and her phobia stayed under control.

"All the same, you couldn't imagine people actually having fun here," she said.

Under a hot August sun the maze was a silent place, dusty and dry despite its greenness. The occasional fly buzzing around their heads, the distant mewing cry of a gull, only deepened the loneliness. Once, a twin-engine plane droned high above, like a visitor from another world. Fleur watched it thoughtfully.

Nothing trailed them, nothing clawed at them from the other side of the hedge. No faces formed in the sprays of yew.

They found nothing but miles of dry turf paths between smugly tidy walls of yew. Paths that spiralled and folded back and looped outward again. And again, and again.

"We've been here before." Fleur stopped and pointed at a broken twig that hung across half their path. "We turned right from here, and there was a dead end."

"Then let's take the left turn, next."

Two bends later, they came to the same dead end. At least, it looked the same.

"And that's it for the twine." Fleur let the end drop. Neil took a notebook from his pack as they retraced their steps.

"We'll start over from the entrance. This time, I'll draw the route. You put down the marbles."

After half an hour he began muttering under his breath. Fleur leaned in for a look and let out a snort of laughter.

"Judging by that, we should be in Amstey by now!"

At four-ten by Neil's watch they collapsed onto the path. Fleur groped in her backpack for an empty root beer can and upended it to get the last warm drop.

Neil knelt to examine a piece of twine that trailed along the ground. The end was frayed as if it had been bitten off.

Next to it stood a small pyramid built of ten white marbles. He glared at this insult, then swept up the marbles and dumped them into his pack.

"You see, I wasn't losing track. They have been moved!"

"And yet I'd swear we're alone in here." She raised her sweating face to catch a breath of air. "Listen!"

There it was again, the sound that had been tormenting them for the last two hours. The music of trickling water. Sometimes it tinkled in the distance, other times it could have been around the next bend.

Now it was so close they could hear the click of tiny stones in the current. You could almost taste that water, cold on the teeth, pure, faintly earthy. Neil licked his dry lips.

"It's playing with us." He climbed to his feet and rubbed his forehead with a grimy hand. "It knows we'll never find the centre, not in a million years."

"D'you think Jasper could tell us, if we asked him?"

"I bet he could! Let's go back to the house and try that sugar trick again."

They had no trouble finding the way out. As they climbed the ridge toward the pines, Neil looked back at the wall of yew. Was it imagination, or did he hear a purr of satisfaction, as if a million twigs were rubbing together?

♋

They stepped into the garden through the lilac hedge in time to see a train of three cars pulling away from the house. The middle one was a gleaming white and wore a hood ornament like the figurehead on a ship. Neil whistled.

The third car was Gregory's. As he followed the others, he waved a V-sign at Neil.

"Looks like good news," Fleur said.

"Yeah. Did you see that car?" For a moment Neil felt cheered. Then he realized what it meant. "Come on, we may not have a lot of time left."

They went into the kitchen by a back door. Fleur opened the refrigerator and brought out a carton of orange juice. Neil lifted two glasses down from the cupboard, then looked for the sugar and something to sprinkle it on.

A mirrored tray leaned against the wall at the back of the counter. It was a rectangle eighteen inches by twelve, with a silver rim and handles. He reached for it, then stopped.

The mirror didn't reflect his hand. Or the room behind him, either. Instead it contained a drifting greyness, like fog.

Then the fog thinned out. A face looked through and caught his eye, and was gone again.

"So that's how he's doing it, this time." Fleur spoke from behind him, over her glass of juice. They crowded together to peer into the mirror. Puffs of mist crawled across its surface. It was like staring into a vat of steaming water.

"But not here," she said firmly. "Outside."

Neil looked around at the kitchen, stale and cold and dark. "You're right. Anywhere but in this house."

He carried the tray out into the courtyard. The house rose all around, the windows like squinting eyes in the shade of the arched walkways. But the sun shone into the centre. Compared to indoors, this was an island of light and air.

Beside the dry marble scallop shell of the fountain stood a white-enamelled iron bench. Its back was shaped like sprays of roses and tulips. Fleur thumped the iron with her knuckle.

"Ouch, try sitting on that!"

Neil leaned the mirror up against the back of the bench and knelt on the brick paving. Fleur crouched beside him. The fog drifted, the face looked out again. Jasper smiled.

"It's getting easier to break through! I must be growing stronger, Neil. More like you."

His hand came up and Neil's hand darted to meet it. And he touched, not cool glass, but the warmth of live skin. Fingertips flexed against his, a perfect match.

"You see? I'm not a ghost!" Jasper's silvery eyes shone. Inside Neil, a wall broke. Wetness blurred his sight. He didn't care if Fleur was watching. All that mattered was the touch of his brother's hand.

"But if you're not a ghost," Fleur was saying, "what are you?"

"Hard to explain." Even the tone of Jasper's voice was familiar, a voice Neil had known all his life, and not just because it was so close to his own. It was a beat quicker, with a hint of a smile in it even when, as now, the face was frowning in thought. "Perhaps you could call me a shade."

"Which means what? A shadow?" Fleur demanded.

"You might say so. I'm partly Jasper's shadow. The only reason I live is because he lived, once. I am who he would have been, if he'd grown. And of course I'm linked to Neil, since we're twins, so you might say I'm his shadow, too."

"Hm." Fleur sat back on the pavement, crossing her legs as if settling in for a nice long chat. "I was going to ask why you grew, instead of staying a baby, but I get it now."

Neil cleared his throat noisily. "It's the link to me."

"That's right. As you grew, I grew. We were always together, even though you couldn't know."

"I never felt it. Or if I did, I thought . . . "

"I know. Imagination. I was sad for you, I wished . . . "

"Me too."

Their hands were still palm to palm. For Neil, who hadn't held anybody's hand since the age of five, the touch was embarrassing. At the same time it was precious, he didn't want to lose it. It was as if a door had opened, spilling out warm air and good smells and happy voices.

"Charlotte!" Fleur knelt up. "Did she grow up too? Is she old now? Or — "

"No, she's still eighteen."

Fleur sank back with a sigh.

"Nothing has changed for her. That's part of the cage she's in. She — "

"I still don't understand," Neil cut in. He was recovering from the shock of joy, and his mind bristled with questions. "I know about your being a shade, but what caused you? Where are you, and how did you get there?"

Jasper blinked. "You caused me."

"Me?"

"Of course. It was your need that called me into being. And Dexter caused me too, though he never had any such intention, when he made the maze. He made a poem about it, about the sort of place it is. Remember?"

"*Shades may live,*" Fleur quoted.

"Just so. Here beyond the maze . . . " He paused and searched for words. "You might find anything. Anything could become real. Because it's a place where nothing is real *yet.*"

"Anything could be . . . " Fleur's eyes went vague, then sharp again. "What's it like — "

Jasper cut in as if he hadn't heard her. "And then there's the blood link with Dexter." His face, colourless like Neil's, grew even paler. "In a way, I'm his shade too."

"No!" Neil's hand tensed. Jasper pushed back at him gently. "I like it no better than you do. But that's the way of it. You and I, and our father too, we're the last of Dexter's blood."

Neil was silent, trying to tell himself it wasn't so.

Jasper's eyes were grey now instead of silver, and he looked thinned-out at the edges. "We have always lived in his shadow. His shadow is *in* us, it's part of us. And we'll stay in his shadow for as long as he rules here, beyond the maze."

He took a breath. His eyes slipped from Neil's and flicked back over his shoulder. Then he moved closer to the mirror's surface and whispered, "Which gives us one more reason to bring him down! And we can do it — together!"

Eleven

Then, let's do it!" Fleur laughed excitedly. "Let's get Dexter, if that's going to help Charlotte." She sprang to her feet, then plopped back. "But how do we get there?"

"Yes," Neil put in, "I still don't understand. You keep talking about this place beyond the maze. Is it under the ground? In the bluff? Where?"

"You see our two hands?" Jasper wiggled his fingertips against Neil's. "The place is as close to you as that. Almost nothing between. And at the same time, it's farther away than the faintest star you can see at night."

"Puzzles!" Fleur wrinkled her nose. "You two sure have a lot in common."

"I think I'm getting it," Neil said slowly.

"Then tell me — in plain English!"

"The maze . . ." He groped toward the idea. "It's a door to another world. Another place."

"I think of it more as a bridge." Jasper grabbed another look over his shoulder. All they could see was billowing fog.

"Something wrong?" Fleur asked.

"Not yet." He turned back and spoke briskly. "The spiral pattern is the key. He discovered it during his travels in eastern lands, but perhaps you've already guessed that. Now, this pattern . . . How shall I put it? It has a way of pushing the stuff the world is made of . . . out of place. It takes a piece of the world and twists until it's not in the same world any more."

He looked at them expectantly. "Clear as mud," Fleur said.

Jasper took a deep breath and pulled his hand away from the mirror. For Neil it was as if the door to the warm room had slammed shut, leaving him out in the cold. But he pretended not to think twice about it.

"Think of your world as being like a ball of bread dough." Jasper shaped a circle with his hands. "If you want to make rolls, you take a small piece and twist it off, isn't that so? Fleur, your father does this: I've seen it through Neil. But suppose you twist a piece almost off, and then leave it there. Do you see?"

Fleur nodded. "The thin, twisted bit in between the big lump and the small one — that's the maze. But why didn't he twist it right off? Why keep the bridge?"

"Good question." Neil sat back on his heels. "He hasn't come back, far as we know. And if the Uglies are working for him, he sure isn't putting out any invitations."

"He has reasons . . . " Jasper shook his head. "I can't tell you all I know. There's so little time left."

Ice touched Neil's stomach. "Are you in danger?"

"We're all in danger. Why do you think you've been watched? We're a threat to Dexter, the three of us, every time we meet. And he has other slaves besides the Nightrunners."

"Nightrunners?" Neil echoed.

"*His* name for them. You call them the Uglies. Keep away from them, I beg you! They aren't what they seem."

Fleur looked around uneasily. The sun had dipped below the roof line. Their island of light had become a well of shadows, ringed around with unseen, hostile eyes.

"Don't worry, there's no danger now. Or at least, not near."
Jasper forced a smile. "It's just that I'm in a hurry. Charlotte
— I don't know how long she can last. She — she's fading."
Fleur scrunched close to the mirror. "What d'you mean?"

"You see, he'll never let her go, now he's got her." Jasper
spoke fast and his eyes were dark and urgent. "And he can
wait as long as he wants. Because time doesn't flow here the
same way it does with you. She's caged up forever and ever,
and she can't bear it any more."

Fleur hugged her arms and watched him, biting her lips.
Neil heard the new sound in Jasper's voice and thought, *He
cares more about her than me.*

"She can't die. But she isn't living, not truly. She doesn't
see me or hear me any more. I think she's only alive now in
her dreams. And I can't help her, because I'm only a shade.
I'm not real!"

Neil reached a hand to the mirror, but Jasper didn't see
and he dropped it. "Don't say that. You're as real as me!"

"No." Jasper's voice fell. He looked at them both. "Only
someone from your world, someone as real as Dexter, can
stand up to him. All I can do is help."

"Well, here we are." Fleur smeared away tears with the
back of her hand. "So what are we waiting for?"

"The way through the maze, of course," Neil said coldly.
"You can bet it won't be easy, even if we get a map."

"True." Jasper watched him with anxious eyes. "There
might be . . . pitfalls. And after you've passed the bridge,
there will be Dexter to deal with. You won't simply be able
to walk out again, with Charlotte. There will be . . . " He
shivered.

"Will be what?" Fleur demanded.

But Jasper was still watching Neil. The happiness of their
meeting was gone. "You won't be sorry if you help," he said

softly. "I know what you want most of all. You want us to be together always."

"Don't you?"

Jasper smiled. "Help Charlotte. Do that, and I'll stay with you forever. You'll never be lonely again."

Neil laughed with sudden joy. He reached to Jasper again, then saw the sadness in his eyes, and began to understand. For the next few seconds he couldn't speak.

"What's with you?" Fleur shook his arm.

He pushed her off. "Jasper thinks I want to be paid. He thinks I wouldn't help Charlotte if he didn't bribe me."

"Well, you can see why," she said reasonably. "Up till now, you've only thought of Jasper. Or the maze. It's been like a puzzle you had to solve. But all he cares about is rescuing Charlotte. Right, Jasper?"

"Can you draw the way through the maze?" Neil heard his voice loud and harsh, and caught Fleur's frown, but didn't care. He avoided Jasper's eyes.

"Spill some salt or sugar, and I'll try. But hurry!"

Neil took the tray by its silver handles and set it flat on the bench, then climbed to his feet. He had taken two steps toward the kitchen when he heard Jasper's cry: "They're coming!" And Fleur's gasp of alarm.

Next moment he was hanging over the mirror. He went cold all over. The fog behind Jasper had turned solid black.

"Run!" Jasper was white and breathless. "Don't wait here, run!"

Neil scrabbled uselessly at the glass. "Come out!"

"I can't! I . . . " He looked back and down. And now Neil could see too. The mirror had become a pit. Straight down through the white iron bench, through air and bricks and earth, into nothingness.

Something was moving, deep in the pit. It grew as it hurtled up at them, but all Neil could see was a boiling blackness. It came on so fast, they had no time to react.

"Get away!" Jasper's white face flashed at them one last time, and the mirror exploded. The air was full of splintered glass.

♋

"If I hadn't kept asking those dumb questions!" Neil shook his hands savagely. Soapsuds sprayed across the kitchen. "If only I'd let him get away sooner! But no, all I could think of was my own dumb self!"

Their last count made it eighteen cuts between them. They had found carbolic soap and plastic Bandaid strips in a first-aid kit under the sink, but a gash under Neil's eye was still oozing. He dabbed at it with a towel.

"He kept telling us he wasn't worried," Fleur said in a muffled voice. She was standing bent over, head downward, gingerly moving a comb through her hair. Another fragment of mirror tinkled to the floor.

"But he was worried, and I should have seen it. I just didn't want to let him go. He might be dead!"

"I don't think you can kill a shade. What worries me is what he's hiding."

"Hiding?"

"Didn't you notice? He hasn't told us everything, that's for sure. I'd like to know what's waiting for us in Dexter's world, that he doesn't want to mention just yet."

"But Jasper's my twin!"

"So?"

"So he's my other half! He'd never try to fool me."

She parted her curtain of hair and looked out at him through it. "You make it sound like he should be wearing a halo. Well, I think he'd do anything for Char — "

"What in the name of — *What happened here?*"

Neil buried his hands in the towel. Fleur straightened up, flinging back her hair. A splinter pinged off the refrigerator behind her. Gregory filled the doorway.

He stepped forward and pulled the blood-stained towel from Neil's arms. "What have you done to yourself?"

"We, uh, broke a mirror."

"It was my fault, Mr. Gunn." Fleur faced him with wide-open blue eyes. "I made Neil take it out to the courtyard where the light was better, and it got broken. We honestly didn't mean it to happen."

Neil avoided staring at her. Amazing, how she managed to tell the truth while leaving out all the important facts!

"Never mind that. Let me look at you." He inspected her arms and face, with their patchwork of pink plastic strips. "Now you." He nudged Neil's face toward the light. Seeing the cut under his eye, he made a hissing sound, and shook his head.

"It's not as bad as it looks," Neil said.

"Half an inch closer . . . Into the car, both of you."

♋

It was two hours later, and the sun was low in the sky, when Neil and his father left the small hospital on the south side of Amstey. Fleur's parents had taken her home as soon as they learned none of her nicks needed treatment.

The doctor had closed Neil's gash with a shiny piece of surgical glue. It felt stiff and peculiar under his eye.

"Don't pick at it," Gregory said. He set the car going along Churchill Avenue and a few minutes later turned in at Super Burger.

Neil ordered a plain burger with no fries. Nervousness had killed his appetite. His father hardly ever got mad, but when he did, the roof shook. He'd been too calm and quiet, there had to be a blast building up.

But when it came, it was surprisingly mild. "Well? That mirror didn't just fall."

"Uh . . . " He concentrated on squeezing ketchup out of a tiny envelope. "Well, maybe I was kind of horsing around. I know, it was dumb. I . . . " He stopped. His father was holding up a hand.

"How many 'small accidents' have you had in the last couple of days? That fall off your bike, that business of the antique desk you broke . . . "

"It was a highboy. But how did you . . . ?"

"The Padgetts had a few words with me," he said dryly. "We'll be splitting the replacement cost. I'm afraid I don't think much of this new friend of yours."

"Fleur? But none of it's her fault!"

"It's not like you to get into scrapes, Neil. The only new factor is Fleur."

And the Uglies, and Dexter, and Jasper, Neil thought. *But I can't tell him that.*

"Well, never mind. We're heading home tomorrow." Gregory took a bite out of his burger.

"Tomorrow! But we can't!"

"The house is sold," Gregory said calmly. "The papers are signed, the new owner takes possession in thirty days."

"Well, then, we could stay a few more days, couldn't we?"

"In that house?" Gregory put down his burger and stared at him. "Neil, it gives you the willies — remember? Me, too, for that matter. What's the real reason?"

Neil took a bite, playing for time. There was nothing he could say that wouldn't sound crazy.

"It's Fleur, isn't it?"

Neil caught his eye. His father was twinkling at him, though he still looked worried. *Fleur?* His face went hot to the hairline. *He thinks . . . Oh, well. At least that's something he'd believe.*

"There are things called telephones," his father said gently. "And letters. And who knows, maybe we'll come back for a visit at Thanksgiving."

"But, Dad . . . "

Gregory was shaking his head. Neil gave up. He knew when he was up against a stone wall.

☉

They drove back to the house. Gregory went into the parlour and turned on the television that sat on a Victorian table, looking completely out of place.

Neil roamed the house, trying to raise Jasper in every mirror he could find. But nothing looked back at him except his own reflection and the image of the room behind him.

He tried pouring sugar on the dark wooden floor of his bedroom. After half an hour of staring at the carefully strewn grains, he got a dust pan and swept it up.

A phone call to Fleur brought the news that her parents were still having fits, and they were starting to think her new friend very odd. What did he think he was doing, playing with mirrors?

"But I'll be there first thing tomorrow. I'll sweet-talk your dad, don't you worry. You won't have to go."

"I won't go. Simple as that." But he knew the defiance was empty. "If only Jasper were here! I'll bet he could talk to my dad. *And* get him to listen!"

The phone was in a cubby hole under the front stairs, to the right of the lobby. The stairs were a wide curve of beige marble, with sea-green spindle railings. Neil started up slowly, trying to think of some other way of reaching Jasper.

Suppose there was no way of reaching him? Suppose it really was possible to kill a shade?

A low, hollow sound distracted him. A windy hooting, like a note played on a pipe organ. He looked around to see what was making it and saw a large vase sitting in a niche in the wall, where the stairs curved up past the corner.

It was two feet high, round-bellied and narrow-necked, and covered with swirling Arabic writing in blue and gold. Gregory had said it was a real Moorish antique, very valuable.

The sound was coming from the vase. Now it reminded Neil of the noise you make by blowing across the mouth of a pop bottle. Only, a pop bottle doesn't talk to you.

"Neil!" it hooted. "Listen! Listen!"

Neil was beside it instantly, his hands on the flaring sides. "Jasper? You're all right!"

"Just listen." The jar vibrated. "We must hurry!"

"My father . . . "

"Meet at a crossroad. Bring Fleur. Midnight tonight."

"Midnight?" Neil hesitated only a second. "Okay! But which crossroad?"

"Doesn't matter," the jar boomed softly. "Any crossroad is a place of meeting. I'll find you. I'll give you the pattern for the maze."

"But the Uglies . . . "

"I'll deal with them. You just come."

"I meant I'm afraid for you!" But the jar under his hands was dead clay, without a quiver. Jasper was gone.

Twelve

A crossroads at midnight," Fleur announced. "Sounds like the perfect time and place to meet a vampire!"

Neil tried to laugh, and shivered instead. "We're here to meet Jasper, not Dracula."

"And besides, I'm wearing my good-luck stone, so we're protected." She waved her left wrist at him, then laughed at his disgusted look.

Well, different people had different ways of pretending they weren't nervous. Clowning was hers. He shifted the straps of his backpack and checked his watch for the tenth time.

They were early. Neil had reached the spot at ten to midnight, Fleur a few minutes later. They propped their bicycles against the HAIG STREET signpost on the northwest corner. They had chosen the intersection of Haig and Highway 21 because it was the crossroads nearest to Fleur's house.

The town of Amstey was asleep. There wasn't a car in sight. "Much trouble sneaking out?" Neil asked.

"I barely made it. Luckily Betts sleeps like a ton of lead, once she does get to sleep. I had to leave the kitchen door unlocked, though, so I hope nobody checks. How about you?"

"No problem. I just walked out."

He looked up and down both roads. They gleamed like a steel cross, cold under the orange tint of the highway lights.

Dead-black shadows lay close to their bases. The drainage ditches were strips of inky nothing.

"I brought this old Etch-Sketch. Think he can use it?" Fleur pulled it from under her arm and twiddled the plastic knobs. Lines ran this way and that across the grey film of the board.

Neil nodded. "Can't hurt to try it. I brought salt, again. Also paper, charcoal and pencils."

The orange light washed out warm skin tones, and turned Fleur's face a sickly greenish-grey. Neil realized he must look the same. *Eerie*. He felt cold, though the night was warm and still.

A sodium light standard rose from one corner of the intersection. Its tall, thin metal body bent over at the neck, its single eye glared through a cloud of moths.

It looked like a hungry ghost. Neil decided not to share this notion with Fleur.

A solitary car went by along Haig. The driver, a woman, peered out at them curiously, then speeded up and vanished around the curve of Sentinel Hill. The engine sound died.

In the stillness, they could hear the sodium light buzzing like a trapped bumblebee. Fleur looked up at it. "I wonder how we're going to explain things like that to Charlotte?"

Neil frowned at her. "Like?"

"That light." She waved up at it. "Not to mention cars, snowmobiles . . . And how would we explain microwave ovens? Or the hole in the ozone layer? Or television? Or space travel? Or that?" She pointed upward.

Paired lights winked overhead as a small plane headed for an airport down south. The drone of its engine faded.

Neil sucked his lip thoughtfully. "Going by what we know of her, I'd guess she'd have no problem with new things. She was the one who wanted to see the world, right? No, the problem will be explaining *her*."

"Why? Oh — I see what you mean. She pops out of nowhere, with no family, not even a birth certificate . . . "

"Or, worse. A birth certificate nobody will believe!"

"One problem at a time. First, we rescue her."

Neil paced back and forth along the edge of the ditch. *Come on, Jasper!*

"Y'know," Fleur began slowly, "I think I've got an idea."

Neil swung his wrist up. "It's one minute to midnight."

"Tell you later, then."

Strange how lonely it was on the empty highway. How dead it looked. Maybe it was the orange light that tricked your eyes.

The shadows in the dry ditch beside him looked like water. From the corner of his eye he saw something stir, but when he looked directly at the ditch he saw nothing.

A bell tolled once, deep and solemn. Then again.

"St. Michael's," Fleur said. They faced toward Sentinel Hill. Fleur counted up as the bongs rolled out. "Nine . . . ten . . . eleven . . . "

"Twelve," said Neil. They held still. After a moment he clenched his hands. "Where is he?"

"Here."

Fleur whirled around. Then laughed at the way she'd jumped. "You made it!"

Jasper stood in the middle of the road behind them, hands in pockets, relaxed. His white T-shirt and black jeans matched Neil's exactly.

Neil was already halfway toward him, hand outstretched. He stopped when they were still a few yards apart. "Are you okay?"

Jasper looked real enough, more solid than he'd looked in the mirror. But he didn't look right, somehow. Neil told himself it was the sodium light that gave him that haggard, hollow-eyed look.

"Of course I am!"

Neil took another step forward. "Can you use a pencil?"

"Bring it to me and I'll try."

He swung his backpack from his shoulders and fumbled with the buckles. He wondered why his hands were shaking.

Fleur held out the Etch-Sketch. "Maybe you should try this first." As Jasper walked toward them, Neil noticed he had no shadow. It gave him a sinking feeling in the pit of his stomach. Fleur noticed it too. Yet what else would you expect?

Jasper saw them both staring at the road behind him, and smiled. It was a secretive smile, more in the eyes than the mouth, more to himself than to them. "You're right. How could a shade have a shadow?"

What's happened to him? Neil wondered. *Why is he different?*

Jasper reached for the Etch-Sketch and then drew back and watched it. It was going crazy in Fleur's hand, dials twisting by themselves, lines zigzagging all over the surface. In a moment it was black with scrawls.

"Fleur, what are you doing?" Neil demanded.

"I'm not doing this!" She held the Etch-Sketch out at arm's length as if it were a snapping turtle. As Jasper reached for it again, it gave a frenzied shake, flew from her hand and smashed on the pavement.

"The thing doesn't like me," he said. He smiled again.

Fleur sidled away from Jasper, back toward Neil. She came up against him with a bump.

Again there was a tiny movement in the ditch. But Neil was too shaken to look, this time. He was shuddering with cold, icy right through to his bones. That was all wrong on a warm summer night like this.

"Neil." Jasper snapped it out like a command. "Let's get on with this. Give me your paper and pencil."

Silently, Neil held them out.

"No. Bring them to me!"

"Wait." Fleur grabbed his arm.

"Bring them, Neil!" Then Jasper dropped his commanding tone and wheedled. "What's wrong? Aren't you glad to see me?"

He stepped toward them. His eyes caught the orange light and reflected it like fire.

Fleur took a sudden quick breath. "Where's Jasper?"

"What do you mean? I'm Jasper!" He spread his arms, all innocence.

"What have you done to him?"

"Touch my hand, Neil." He held it out. "Feel me: I'm real."

"Don't," Fleur muttered. "Whatever he says to do, *don't do it.*"

Neil didn't need the advice. His mouth was cinder-dry with fear.

"You weren't afraid to touch my hand in the mirror, Neil." Again the piteous tone. But the eyes were still burning. He took another step toward them.

Neil suddenly flung his pad of paper, hoping to distract the other. To give them a few seconds' running time.

But the boy — if it was a boy — flicked a hand and the pages streamed from the pad in midair, one after the other. Up and around they whirled, like leaves caught in a tornado.

Then the storm of paper was in their faces, beating at their heads. Sharp corners sliced at Neil's cheeks; he covered his eyes and stumbled backward.

His heels tilted. They were on the brink of the ditch, where the inky shadows lay. Suddenly the paper storm was over. Pages whitened the ground. Only a few still fluttered in the air. Fleur glanced back over her shoulder and Neil heard her gasp. He looked back too. For a few moments he couldn't move or think.

The puddles of shadow were breaking up. Shapes were surfacing from them like swimmers from a lake. A long hand with twig-skinny fingers reached out and scrabbled at the ground. Pointed nails scraped in the dirt.

All Neil could do was stare. *It isn't real. This is a nightmare.*

An elbow poked up, scraggy and sharp. Then a bony shoulder; then a huge back that uncurled, horribly like a grub. Darkness dripped from it as it straightened up.

Finally the blurred head unbent and looked up at him. A gash of mouth opened across the face. It had no eyes. There was no light in it anywhere: it was all shadow.

Swaying on hands and knees, it crept out of the patch of darkness toward Neil and Fleur. Others crawled up behind it from the black depths.

Neil's heart thudded three times while this happened. Then Fleur grabbed his wrist and yanked. They jumped away from the ditch, then turned together, ready to run, and found they were facing the boy with the burning eyes.

He smiled in that secret way, behind his eyes, though his mouth was grave. "You were warned. You didn't listen."

Neil shook off Fleur's hand. *I'll have to fight him. There's no other way out.* But the marrow of his bones screamed No! He — it — was worse, far worse than the crawling shadows.

"Don't touch him!" Fleur grabbed his arm and dragged him back.

"Got to!" The first of the shadows was climbing the bank. He knew it by the wave of cold on his legs.

"Come to me, Neil." The boy laughed softly. "Touch my hand. We'll be one, you and I. Forever and ever!"

Neil crouched, hands spread, the way he'd seen it done in movies. Somewhere not far away, a car horn blared, but he ignored it. He took a step forward. Then another. The boy smiled.

Thin fingers closed around Neil's ankle. He yelled and kicked backward.

Then a roaring sound swept over them. A blinding white light sliced across the cold orange glow and caught the boys in its glare. Rubber squealed on asphalt.

Gregory ducked out of the car. "I thought you'd come this way. Neil, this puts the lid on it. What kind of crazy . . . "

He strode towards them, and then he saw the boy. He stopped. "Dad," Neil said quietly, "let's get away." Fleur reached for Gregory's arm, but he brushed her hand aside and took another step forward. His eyes went from Neil to the other and back again.

"I'm your son," said the boy with the burning eyes. "I'm Jasper." He held out a hand. "Touch me! I'm real."

"No, Dad!"

Gregory reached for the outstretched hand. Neil put his head down and charged. Mid-leap, he saw the hands touch. Too late!

Thirteen

Neil hit the pavement hard and lay winded. He was still dragging air back into his lungs as he rolled over and scrambled to his feet.

In the white glare of headlights he saw his father lying face down, one arm outstretched. Fleur knelt beside him. The three of them were alone. In the ditches, the shadows lay flat.

Gregory hadn't moved. Neil's chest went icy. He dropped to his knees and grabbed at the limp, heavy shoulders. The head flopped to and fro. "Dad! Dad!"

Neil went on shouting and shaking him till other hands pushed him off and a voice yelled in his ear.

"He's not dead!"

Not dead. The meaning finally got through to him. He sat back on his heels. "But he's . . . not . . . waking up." It was hard to talk, his throat was so tight.

A heavy engine rumbled in the distance. Slowly it grew louder. By the time another set of headlights swung across them, Fleur was out in the middle of the highway, jumping up and down and waving her arms.

☙

At noon the next day Neil was sitting on a hard vinyl chair, staring at a door in a hospital corridor. Too tired to sit upright, he hunched forward with his forearms braced on his thighs.

Fleur sat beside him, sipping apple juice from a bottle through a straw. She'd brought him a bottle too, but it sat unopened on the floor under his chair.

She had changed into white cotton pants, a loose turquoise shirt and clean sneakers. The sleeves and pant legs hid most of her bandages, all except one on the neck and one on the cheek. She had replaced the plain pink strips with fancy ones, bright blue with silver stars.

Two gold combs held her hair back from her face. As always, the pearly oval hung on a chain about her left wrist. She was sparkling and cheerful. In fact, much too cheerful. As if his dad wasn't lying behind that door, blank as a wiped chalkboard.

Neil was still wearing the jeans and T-shirt he'd worn the day before. Both were smeared with road dirt. The shirt was also dotted with rusty bloodstains, from when the mirrored tray had exploded, and the jeans were greenish on the knees and rear end, from their last visit to the maze.

"He's going to be all right, you know," said a voice. Neil looked up and tried to smile at the doctor.

"Is he awake?"

"Not yet." Her eyes were large and dark, but sharp. They probed all over his face and clothes as if he were one of her patients. "Who won the fight?"

"I did," Fleur said. The doctor didn't laugh.

"Just a small accident," Neil put in. "How's my dad?"

"Well, it's a puzzle. He hasn't had a heart attack or stroke. But he's in severe shock. Are you sure? . . . "

"Nothing happened," he said firmly. *Nothing you'd believe, anyway*, he added mentally.

"We'll keep monitoring him. If it's simple shock, he'll begin to recover soon. In the meantime . . . " She pursed her lips. "We'll have to make arrangements for you."

"Oh, that's okay," Fleur said brightly. "He can stay with us."

"In that crowded house of yours, Fleur?" Now the doctor laughed. "I'd better phone your parents and make sure."

"Waste of time," Neil muttered as she walked away along the corridor. "I'm surprised they even let you come to the hospital."

"They almost didn't. Till I told them how you and your dad were having problems. That explained why we were all out on the highway."

"Problems? I don't get it."

"Well, I sort of hinted you were thinking of running away . . . Don't look like that! It got my mother on your side. She's about ready to adopt you."

Neil said nothing as he stooped to pick up his bottle of juice. *Just wake up, Dad. Just get better.*

Wheels rattled. A man in white clothes pushed a steel trolley past them. It was stacked with covered dishes and smelled of hot beef gravy.

"Come on." Fleur pulled at his arm. "You had no breakfast, you must be hungry."

"No."

"Okay, but it's time we got out of here."

"I can't leave my dad."

"You mean you're just going to sit here like a lump and do nothing to help him?" She stood up and hoisted her backpack. It sagged heavily from her shoulders. Neil glared up at her.

"I mean it," she said sharply. "Dexter's got him. Just like he's got Jasper and Charlotte. Sitting and feeling bad won't do him one bit of good, or them either."

He gripped the juice bottle tight, to keep himself from throwing it. "So what will?"

"Don't ask. Trust me." She winked.

"You've figured out the way?" He stood up, excited.

"I said don't ask!" She turned and headed briskly along the corridor toward the stairs. Maddened with curiosity, knowing he was doing exactly what she meant him to do, he left the unopened bottle on the chair and followed.

♋

Amstey's small hospital lay on the south edge of town, among new, bright yet flimsy-looking buildings. Fleur held Neil by the arm and steered him westward along Churchill Avenue, past the curling arena, the community centre and Super Burger. The lake spread its soft glitter at the end of the street.

As they walked, a tinny musical sound grew louder. Suddenly Fleur pulled him toward a gate in a chain link fence. "Here we are!"

A ticket booth stood in the gateway with AMSTEY HARVEST FAIR blazoned on a big sign on its roof. Neil stopped dead.

"A fair? Why would I want to see a fair?"

"Well, I'll admit the farm show isn't much. You know: the biggest zucchini in the county, the fattest pig, the best buckwheat. But there's a good midway. Me and my friends go every year. And the chili dogs — mm, mm!" She smacked her lips.

"You expect me to fool around on a midway while my dad . . . " Neil broke off. It struck him that Fleur was being far too bouncy, even for her. She was almost like a cartoon of herself.

She was at his arm again, nudging him toward the ticket booth. He pulled away. "What are you up to?"

"Don't ask questions!" Her eyes flashed at his, suddenly not cheery at all. "This is something I thought of last night. I don't want to talk about it."

"But — "

"I don't even want to *think* about it. Remember the Uglies? How they might be able to read our minds? Well, they could be around. So do us a favour, okay? Just enjoy yourself for once! Anyway, you could use a break."

As she gabbled on she was pushing him at the booth. He gave in and pulled out his wallet. "First stop," she said when they were through the turnstile. "Lunch!"

Smells filled the air. Smells of onions and potatoes frying in stale fat, of cotton candy and caramel corn, of warm asphalt, of machine oil. And the aroma of manure from a shed nearby, with a sign: AGRICULTURAL EXHIBITS.

Neil's mouth tightened. When Fleur urged him over to a food stall and insisted on buying him a back bacon, fried onion and green pepper sandwich, his stomach lurched.

"Eat! You'll feel better. Food always helps, my gran says." She bit into her chili dog.

The bacon sandwich oozed fat. He closed his eyes, took a bite and forced it down. By a miracle, it stayed down. A moment later he did feel better. His stomach grew steady. He noticed that the sun shone, a breeze blew and people were smiling.

He still felt guilty when he thought of his father, but he finished the sandwich.

Past the kiddie rides, they were into the uproar of the midway. Every booth blared out competing music. A few yards away, the roller coaster rumbled and a giant cage whirled screaming people upside down and sideways.

Fleur bought a strip of tickets. "Just in case," she said.

She sauntered along, pointing and exclaiming between bites of her chili dog. Neil paid a dollar to shoot at wooden ducks, and missed each time. Fleur threw darts at balloons, and won a silver cowboy hat with a long, curling black feather in the band. She waved it at a cluster of boys and girls who were lining up for the ferris wheel.

"Fleur! Where've you been lately?"

"Around!" she yelled back.

"Friends?" Neil asked. "You want to go with them?"

"Nope." Jamming the silver hat on her head, she veered toward a cotton candy booth. She came back with a plastic bag of what looked like pink fibreglass insulation. Neil pulled off a wisp and let it melt in his mouth.

"You ready to tell me what's going on?"

"Too busy having fun!" She shifted her backpack on her shoulders. It looked heavy. He put out a hand.

"Want me to carry — "

"No. Let's go!" She was off again, dancing through the crowd in her summery clothes, laughing back at him, talking non stop.

"How's your aim? Want to throw footballs at the hoop? Or pennies at milk bottles? Though I've heard there's a trick to that, they just bounce out. Oh, look, here's those digger machines where you try to grab prizes . . . "

She skidded to a stop. Neil bumped into her, and the oncoming stream of people parted around them.

"What is it?" He tried to step past her, but she pulled him back.

"Look!"

Through a gap in the crowd, he saw a big-shouldered figure in dark green stooped over a tent cable, as if checking the fastening. Neil shuffled backwards, pushing Fleur, but it was too late. A round head turned. In the band of shadow under a peaked cap, eyes met his and lit up with a yellow gleam.

"Down!" Fleur whispered. She turned and ran, half crouched, back the way they'd come. He scuttled after her. People stopped and stared.

They darted between two booths and around to the rear, then doubled back. They picked a way between garbage cans and tangles of thick electrical cables. At each gap between the tents and booths they peered out at the crowd.

"Looks like we've lost him," Neil said breathlessly. "Now, d'you mind telling me what we're doing here?"

"Don't make me think of it!" Fleur hissed over her shoulder. "It'll bring him. Make your mind a blank."

"My mind's never a blank!"

"Okay, then think of the gate. Think of us leaving."

"Because we're not?"

"Bingo!" She sidled along a canvas wall. "Come on out, I really think we've . . . Oh, no."

Between them and the midway stepped a figure pushing a broom, a dark silhouette on the sunlit crowd beyond. He dropped the broom with a clatter and stumped towards them. They turned and ran.

Around the back of the next tent, out onto the midway again. "They move slow," Neil panted. "All we have to do is outrun . . ."

Yards ahead, on the right, a clumsy shape in dark green edged through the crowd towards them, bent under the bulk of two big garbage bags. Nobody else noticed him any more than a rock in a stream.

"Fleur! Over here!" A girl waved from the roller coaster lineup. Fleur streaked past.

Neil had to stretch his stride to keep up. "Some . . . place . . . with two . . . exits!"

"There!" They pounded up to the House of Horrors. Then Fleur swerved away from it. The lineup stretched for ten yards. Taped moans and real screams faded behind them as they dashed on. The Indy Race Tunnel was popular too.

But the Fun House seemed to have been forgotten. Maybe it was the childish cartoons daubed in faded colours on the walls, that made it look so stupid and dull. It could have been left over from when their parents were young. No electronics, no laser lights, no special effects. Not even music.

And no line-up. Fleur pushed a couple of tickets at the woman sitting on the steps and leaped up past her through a curtain of grimy plastic strips. Neil swept one last glance around, then followed. The curtain rustled together behind them. They stood still, blinded.

Cold fingers curled into Neil's. Fleur's breathing was loud near his ear. "Not such a good idea," she muttered.

Fourteen

By the way sound came back to him, Neil knew they were in a cramped space. He reached out and touched fabric-covered surfaces on two sides, emptiness in front. "This way. Slide your feet."

They shuffled forward, and found the end of the passage by bouncing off it. It was sheathed in rubber. A dim blue glow showed an opening to the right. They stepped through and found just enough light to see their way.

Neil let go of Fleur's arm and forged ahead eagerly. A figure in a dirty white T-shirt rushed at him and he flinched back. So did the other person.

"Mirrors!" He'd forgotten what was in a place like this, if he'd ever known.

"Feel your way," Fleur whispered. "And don't let's get split up! If I have to stay in here much longer, I'll scream my head off."

"Don't! The Uglies'll hear. If they find out where we are, all they'll have to do is watch the exits."

"Shh!"

They stood still, listening. Their reflections stared back at them, pale and huge-eyed in the hazy blue glow. They looked like frightened strangers, one of them wearing a silver hat with a long black plume.

A step or two behind stood another pair, with their backs turned. Beyond them, another pair, facing the right way. And back beyond them . . .

Fleur moved her head, and a long row of silver hats moved and gleamed. "There's miles of us!" she whispered.

The wooden floor creaked as heavy feet moved along the entry passage behind their backs. They looked at each other nervously. Just another ordinary human being, probably. Or maybe not.

Neil stepped softly to the right, then stopped as his reflection jumped at him again. No way through here. They tiptoed back and forth, sweeping their hands up and down the walls. Solid glass wherever they touched.

"We took a wrong turn." Neil started back the way they'd come. Then jerked to a halt. Around the far corner of the passage came a slinking dark shape, flanked by an army of reflections.

Not one of the Uglies. Or was it? He didn't stop to study it. He was too busy scrambling to keep up with Fleur.

Only one way to go, and it lead nowhere. They jostled into the end of the passage, a corner full of broken images. Hard nails scraped the floor behind them. Neil was turning to protect his back when Fleur shrieked, "Yes!"

She hurled herself at the mirror. And vanished.

Neil gaped. Then jumped after her and found himself in another passage set at a sharp angle to the first. One of those solid walls had been a reflection.

Fleur was gone. Using his outstretched hands as guides, he moved as fast as he could. A clump of black ferns sprouted ahead of him at eye level. He froze, then realized it was Fleur's feather, poking out from wherever she was standing, and reflected a dozen times.

"Get moving!" he whispered. The ferns flipped out of sight.

Another two turns, and he caught up to her. The slinking shape hadn't shown up again, but pattering noises came from somewhere behind them. And someone was breathing loudly nearby. Neil thought it might be himself, but he wasn't sure.

"We're really lost now," Fleur murmured.

He nodded. "Lost in another maze. And not thinking straight." He pushed his mind back, trying to retrace the way they'd come, but the angled mirrors had taken away his sense of direction.

They found their way more by sound than sight. By listening for stealthy noises and trying to move away from them. In this dim, blue, endless place, sight was too confusing.

"This is worse than if it was totally dark," Neil whispered.

The first distorting mirror nearly wrecked things for them. Neil stepped cautiously around a corner and came face to face with a mushroom-headed monster, mouth and eyes stretched wide in a squashed face. His yell bounced off the hard walls around them and ran away in all directions.

"It's you, idiot!" Fleur muttered. A mob of footsteps began to scurry behind them. They dropped caution and ran, and their thousand reflections ran with them. Fleur's hat flew off and rolled along the floor.

Neil lost count of the number of times he slammed into walls that looked like air. Fleur, a step or two behind, at least had his crashes to warn her.

He didn't mind the bruises so much as the faces. They peered slyly out at him from the angles of the mirrors, at times only half showing, or else doubled and tripled.

Sharp teeth gleaming, long ears pricked, eyes not quite animal and not quite human. He was never sure whether they shared the space he moved in — Fleur didn't act as if she saw them — but wherever they were, they were too close for comfort.

And among the long lines of faces that moved with his, were some that looked like his, but weren't. Once he saw his father gazing at him sternly. Once he caught sight of Jasper — it had to be Jasper! — his eyes shining eagerly, his mouth shaping the word *hurry!*

And once, looking right back at him from inches away, a cold, handsome face full of secret laughter.

"Fleur. Did you? . . . " They'd stopped to catch their breath and listen. He was going to ask her if she'd seen what he'd seen, because if she hadn't, he was going crazy.

Then he saw how pale she was. This box with no way out had to be like a bad dream for her, even worse than the maze.

"You okay?"

"Right as rain," she said grimly.

A minute later, they came upon a few scraps of silver on the floor. More lay farther on. They were all that was left of Fleur's cowboy hat. Sharp nails had shredded it. Fleur looked at the scraps and her pale face took on a greenish tinge.

Then Neil realized. "We've come in a circle."

"We're never getting out of here."

"Sure we are. Turn right next time instead of left."

They walked on. The maze all around them was alive with footsteps.

At last, a blind passage. This time it was no mirror trick: it was a real dead end. Fleur leaned her head against the glass, exhausted. Neil stood looking back, every nerve on edge. The footsteps were definitely nearer.

"Fleur, this is a trap. We've got to move."

She still leaned against the panel. He peered at her. Had she gone to sleep standing up?

Then, with a triumphant *ah-hah*, she set her hands one above the other on the mirror, crooked her fingers and pulled.

White brilliance cracked across the blue. Another pull, and Fleur fell outward into a blaze of daylight.

Neil fell out after her. He landed three feet down and sprawled on turf. As soon as he was out, Fleur swung the panel shut, taking care to make no noise. If this was the back door, the Uglies hadn't discovered it yet.

Neil got his breath back. "How did you know — "

"Didn't. Saw the hinges at the last second." She grinned at him in triumph.

He laughed back at her, suddenly full of energy again. The sunlight was a dazzling gold. He felt he'd just woken up from a nightmare of drowning.

He looked at his watch. "Fifteen minutes. That's how long we were in there."

"It felt like a week!"

"Better not wait around."

They scrambled to their feet. Wooden walls rose on both sides. When they ran to the front of the alley, they saw no sign of the Uglies. The woman on the steps sat there alone. Fleur hitched up the straps of her backpack. "Now!"

This time Neil knew enough to ask no questions. Fleur led the way at a fast walk through the crowd, which thinned out as they left the midway behind. They crossed a strip of parkland. The lake spread out ahead of them. Just above the beach lay a wide stretch of concrete.

Fleur waved her arm grandly. "There!" she announced. "There's the reason why we came to the fair." She beamed.

A smile spread across Neil's face. "Smart!"

"I thought so."

It was a giant dragonfly. Body and nose mostly glass, framed in white steel. Long orange tail. Two thin blades like wings sprouted from the roof.

The pilot was already in his seat, they could see him through the large front window. Two women in bright print dresses were walking toward the helicopter, after handing money to a boy who stood at the edge of the pad, under a sign advertising BOB'S HELICOPTER SERVICE — SEE YOUR TOWN FROM THE AIR — RIDES $25 PER PERSON, INCLUDES TAX.

Fleur gritted her teeth in frustration. "There's people ahead of us!"

"Only two. You can see there's room for four, plus the pilot. But, wait a minute. Twenty-five bucks each!"

She started to run, at the same time swinging her pack off her shoulders. "I broke my piggy bank. You can owe me. Told you I had this in mind since last night, didn't I? When I saw that plane flying over I remembered the maze, and — "

"You pay here," said the boy in a bored tone. Fleur dumped her pack on the ground, dug into it and came up with a fistful of bills and coins. She counted out a ten, five fives and seven twos. Then a loonie from her pocket. Neil grabbed her pack and they were running again.

The pilot grinned at them as they climbed in through the open door. "Get belted in, kids!"

The two women turned frizzy heads, one grey, one white, to look back over their seats. Two pairs of pale blue eyes sparkled. "Isn't this fun?" they twittered.

Next moment the floor was vibrating under their feet and a rhythmic hum filled the air. Excitement fizzed through Neil's veins. Then the ground dropped away below, and for a moment his stomach went with it.

But he had no time to feel sick. There was too much to see. From the air Amstey looked so different, so tidy and small and perfect, like a model landscape. The bit of parkland below them was a strip of green velvet beside a blue silk lake. On the other side the midway was a jumble of colours and shapes.

Then the midway slid back, and the helicopter was flying north. Fleur groped in her pack and pulled out a pair of binoculars. "Borrowed these from good ol' Rick." She shoved them into Neil's hand. Then she dived in again, pulled out a small camera and checked the settings.

"Oh, Mother, look!" cried one of the ladies in front. "There's the town hall. And there's the war memorial!"

"Oh, and there's the harbour. Isn't it all so exciting!"

Neil hardly heard them. He was mesmerized by this new view of Amstey as it unrolled beneath. Instead of the faces of buildings, all he could see was roofs, and the patterns of streets and roads as they curled out from Queen's Circle. The spirals, crossed by straights, looked like a spider's web

No: two spiders' webs, one north of the other. The second one swirled out from the top of Sentinel Hill.

"There's my house!" Fleur yelped in his ear. He nearly dropped the binoculars.

"Oh! Where?" cried the ladies in unison.

"Right across from the church. See the park? See, there's my skylight! Oh, yikes, you can see *in!*"

A moment later they were skimming above the streets that looped across the north side of the hill. Then the double spiral of Amstey was left behind, and cornfields floated below them. Cars on the highway were ladybugs running along a thread.

Suddenly Neil saw familiar ground to the left of the highway: a hill, a band of dark trees, a meadow. Fleur held her camera poised. Neil focused the binoculars.

Beyond the meadow the ground rose again and there lay the maze, but from here you could only see swirling lines. The pattern was still hidden.

Then the ground tilted and slid away to the right, taking the maze with it. "Hey!" Fleur protested. "Fly straight!" But the pilot held to his new course, south along the lake shore.

"This is where I turn, kids."

Neil leaned forward against his seat belt. "But we've hardly seen anything! Please can't we go back?"

"Sorry. You want a special route, you pay extra."

"But I've spent all my money!" Fleur slumped back in her seat. "Fifty bucks for nothing!"

Neil took a look back. The maze was already out of sight. They'd crossed Haig Street and now the spiral streets of Sentinel Hill lay below, with a glint of gold, the cross on top of St. Michael's, marking the centre.

Funny to think how Amstey had two centres, just the way Jasper had described the maze. The northern centre, where Fleur lived, even had a spring in it: that fountain in the park. Just like the . . . Just like . . .

"Fleur!"

"What?" She was still slumped morosely in her seat.

"Look down."

"Why?"

"Just look!"

She looked. For a moment she blinked downward dully, then her breath stopped and she pressed her face to the glass.

"Oh . . . my . . . holy . . . "

Below lay the long curve of Circle Road, ringing the base of the hill and feeding into Harbour Street. Then the wide L-shape of Lakeshore Road and Gunn Streets. And then Victoria Avenue peeled off from Gunn, and curled southward. And at last the tightening spirals led into Queen's Circle. The second centre.

The false centre.

Fleur was still glued to the window. "I could kick myself!" she whispered fiercely. "All my life I've been walking the hugest maze there ever was, and I never knew!"

Fifteen

The two ladies were still twittering contentedly as the helicopter touched down, but Neil and Fleur were silent. Fleur's eyes shone like sapphire.

"A map," Neil said, as they crossed the landing pad. "Can you believe that guy? He made the whole town into a map of the maze! Didn't I tell you he was laughing at everybody?"

"But a lot of streets are new since Dexter's day. That makes the pattern hard to see."

"If we could find his original plan . . . "

"I know exactly where." Fleur knuckled the side of her head. "Talk about dense! We've both seen it, only two days ago."

Neil remembered. "After what happened then, you think Mr. Venables is going to let us through the door?"

"Sure he will." Fleur was keeping a sharp lookout as they trotted out through the back gate of the fairgrounds. "I brought the magazines and letters back this morning. He took the magazines, then he gave me back the letters. He said, 'Give these to your parents, I'm sure they never meant to let them go.' He's okay."

♋

"It's still on the table back there." Mr. Venables nodded towards the back of the shop, then hurried off to hover around a customer. They found the book where they'd left it, and Fleur flipped the pages until she found the map.

"The answer was right there in front of our eyes." She shook her head, disgusted with herself. "Why couldn't I *see?*"

Neil's trembling finger traced the route across the page. "Because it doesn't show all the paths. It's not a plan of the whole maze, it's just the two main routes. To the two centres. That's why it was hard to recognize."

"You're right about Dexter." Fleur shook her head, almost in awe. "He's been laughing at the whole town!"

"See? Along here." Neil's finger touched the long straight line of Lakeshore Road. "That's the middle path from the entrance. Gunn Street is where it branches off to the right, and that's where we got into the spiral leading to the false centre."

"So we should have passed Gunn and gone on to Harbour, sort of. And then turned left."

"You can see where the street turns into the last circle," Neil murmured, "up here on the top of Sentinel Hill. That looks so familiar . . . "

"I'm sure we've been there!" Fleur jigged from foot to foot. "In the maze, I mean. That's where the sound of water was the loudest."

"So there must be a way through! Unless . . . "

"Unless this is another trick."

They stared at each other tensely. But Neil knew. His bones knew. "No, this is it."

Fleur pulled a notebook and marker out of her pack and started to copy the plan.

"That'll take too long." Neil could hardly stand still. His backbone was twitching, his neck prickling. He sensed the enemy closing in.

"Maybe, but I don't see a photocopier around here. And we can't count on remembering all the twists and turns. My guess is, we'll run into a few tricks before we reach the true centre."

She took five minutes over the job. As she finished, the door closed behind the customer and Venables walked over.

"What's in the wind? By the look of you, you've stumbled on the end of the rainbow."

"Well, it's . . . sort of a treasure hunt." Fleur drew the last circle and slapped her notebook shut. "Um . . . thanks." She stood awkwardly a moment, fussing with her pack.

Neil knew how she was feeling. Venables had been more patient with them than they deserved. Now he'd helped them out a second time, yet they couldn't repay him with the truth.

"We'll tell you all about it," Neil said. "When we can."

"I'll hold you to that." He cocked his head at them like a sparrow. "Well, whatever you're up to, be careful!"

"We will!" they chorused.

They burst out the door in a jangle of chimes, hit the street and started running. A long trip lay ahead and their bikes were at Fleur's house.

Four blocks north and east of the antique shop, they dropped onto the steps of Knox Presbyterian to catch their breath and wipe sweat from their eyes. Church Street climbed the hill ahead, a long stretch of hot cement in the afternoon sun. All the way up to the top . . .

"Boy, could I use a cold drink." Neil leaned back into the shade of the deep stone doorway.

Fleur looked back past him. Her eyes closed briefly, then opened again, wide. "Don't get comfy!"

He glanced back along Church Street. At the turn, where two banks faced each other, a pair of dark figures came into view. Stumping along in their odd, stiff-legged way, but making good time.

Neil and Fleur heaved themselves off the steps and jogged on up Church Street, puffing and sweating. Finally, left onto Summit Road, around the crescent to Park Circle. Across the little round park. Almost there . . .

Fleur staggered and bent double. "Ugh! Stitch!"

Neil darted back, grabbed her by the arm and pulled her after him. He could see their bicycles in a driveway two houses along. The bikes had been moved to clear a path for the red Corvette that was backing out onto the road.

"Rick!" Fleur screamed. She unbent and sprinted.

♋

They clung to the new-smelling scarlet upholstery as the car swooped down the north side of Sentinel Hill. From Haig the Corvette turned left onto the highway, and Rick put his foot down. He passed other cars with a satisfying *whump* of air.

"Serious stuff, eh?" He chuckled.

"Very serious, Richard." Fleur sat beside him, holding her notebook in both hands and jiggling with impatience.

Neil sat in back, watching through the rear window. They'd lost the Uglies again. At least, he hadn't seen any dark pickup truck creeping up behind.

Yet he hadn't lost that feeling of someone breathing down his neck. If anything, it was stronger.

Rick let them out in the circular driveway in front of the Gunn house. Fleur left her pack in the car and set off at a dead run. Neil yelled "Thanks!" over his shoulder, then he was after her. Across the garden, through the gap in the lilac hedge, across the meadow of long grass and up the pine ridge.

Up and over, and down, heels skidding in the sandy soil. A squish in the rivulet at the bottom, then up again. Not tired any more, plenty of breath to run, now that the hill's yew crown was only a few yards above.

Still in the lead, Fleur tossed a laughing glance back at him. "Come on, snail!"

We're going to make it! Neil exulted. And then he stumbled to hands and knees as the ridge to the south rose into view. Over the brow of the hill from the town came two, then three — no, more — dark figures, clumsily running. Fleur saw them too.

"They didn't bother with the truck." Neil scrambled up. "How'd they get here so fast? How many are there?"

"Never mind, we're still way ahead. They're so clumsy, they'll never catch up!"

More figures came shambling over the ridge. They stood milling together, then they were down on the ground, wriggling.

"What the heck are they doing?" Fleur squinted.

"Getting out of their overalls." But it was more than that. They were like snakes shedding old skins.

It only took seconds. As soon as the overalls were off the Uglies were up and running — on all fours. Neil couldn't stop staring.

The clumsiness was gone. Their massive shoulders and short legs no longer looked odd or deformed. They flashed down the hill with fluid speed, their bodies stretching out, like huge greyhounds.

Fleur leaped for the maze. Neil hared after her.

He had never run so fast in his life. There was no time to stop and look at their map. Good thing he'd stared so hard at it, it was printed on his brain.

They passed the turnoff to the false centre in seconds. Turned left at the next branch so fast, they both skidded and piled up against the elastic boughs of the hedge, which flung them off again.

They bounced up and ran, ran, ran. The path curved north, then to the right, away from the sun, then back toward it, and Neil knew they must be running a complete circuit. *Please don't let us end up where we started!*

No. Fleur, in front, slithered to a halt. This branch in the path was new. She opened her notebook and they bent their heads together over it. "That's where we've been." Neil traced a circle and tapped the spot on the page. "We must be here."

"So we go straight on. If we're still on track, we'll soon come to a sharp right."

He nodded, then raised his head to listen. For the moment everything was quiet. A breeze cooled his sweaty forehead. Fleur flapped her damp shirt and pushed back the hair that kept sliding over her face. It could have been any hot, drowsy summer afternoon.

Then a cry drifted to them on the breeze. An animal cry, a high-pitched squalling without words. There was an eager excitement in it.

Fleur went pale. "They smell us. They know where we are."

"Then let's get going." He didn't add his thought, that when they got to the centre there would be no place else to go. That they might be running head first into a trap.

A few yards farther on they came to the sharp right turn. Farther still, another branching-place. "The map gives two routes from here," she said. "Left looks shorter."

They turned left. It took them on another clockwise circuit inside the first. As they ran along the curving path, a chorus of yips and squeals broke out beyond the hedge to their left. Breath hissed through teeth, paws hit the path. Then, with chilling speed, the sounds of the hunt were past.

They're one lap behind and closing in. Neil didn't have to say it. Fleur put her head down and sprinted.

She ran straight into the end of the passage and bounced back with a yell. Her notebook fell to the ground.

Neil pounced on it. Fleur pawed the page open. "We're here!" She stabbed at the spot. "The last circle should be opening right here!" On the Amstey map, it was the place where Summit Road met Park Circle.

It was a blind alley. Eight-foot walls of yew rose on three sides. You couldn't climb them without a ladder, you couldn't get through without an axe.

"Why didn't I take a hatchet to it in the first place?" Neil was hot with anger at himself.

"Because you thought it'd be easy to get in."

"No. I knew it would be hard. It was a puzzle I had to solve. How stupid could I get!"

A howl of excitement, off to the west. The pack had come to the sharp right. They knew they were close.

Fleur pushed at the hedge in front of her. The thick yew needles pushed back. "It's got to be here!"

"It doesn't," Neil said savagely. He was watching the open end of the path, where the Uglies would appear. "It's one of Dexter's jokes."

"Maybe it's like the mirrors in the Fun House. Looks solid but isn't." She tried walking straight into the hedge, only to flinch back. "Ow! But Jasper said — "

"Maybe Jasper's one of Dexter's jokes, too." He knew he had to be desperate, to say that. At this moment, he was utterly beaten. Trapped and betrayed.

"No. Jasper said there's a way through and I believe him. Dexter's hidden it, that's all." She scowled around at the hedge walls.

"Then how do we find it? Quick!"

Too late. The hunt swept around the corner, a mob of hunchbacked beasts, heads low, legs blurred with speed. They didn't pause. Human-sounding screams of triumph broke from them.

Fleur's hand found Neil's. They backed against the hedge. The last thing Neil saw was the blazing yellow eyes of the leader as it sprang.

Sixteen

Neil shut his eyes and made it all disappear.

He knew and saw and felt nothing. Not the jaws of the beast-men, not the hand wringing his, not the needles prickling through the back of his T-shirt.

Darkness took him. He sank down and down through the cool depths.

♋

Then, like a slap on the back, sunshine. A crushing pain in his hand. He opened his eyes and found he was looking *into* the hedge instead of away from it.

Fleur dropped his hand and whipped around. The Uglies were nowhere to be seen.

"We're through!" She leaned limply against the elastic boughs and let them cradle her.

"But how?" Neil stared around.

"Terror?" Fleur pushed away from the hedge.

"So it was an illusion, that piece of the hedge." He gave her a nod. "Like you said."

"Darn good illusion, too." She twisted off a needle and crushed it with her thumbnail. A sharp, piney scent rose up. "It must be why nobody's found the true centre before." She tilted her head. "Listen!"

"I don't hear anything."

"Not even the Uglies?"

Then Neil understood. You'd expect to hear a lot of frustrated yelping and scratching on the other side of the hedge. There wasn't even a snuffle. He stretched, suddenly light and ready to move.

"Oh, great." Fleur flicked the yew needle away. "I've left the map back there!"

"Never mind, I don't think we'll need it now."

She held out her hand, and Neil surprised himself by taking it without hesitation. He wasn't normally the hand-holding type. But as they walked forward together, he knew: this was not a normal place. He needed a friend's touch as much as she did.

Everything was different. The sky was an evening amber, when it should have been an afternoon blue. The air held that hush of the moment just after the sun has gone, leaving most of its light behind.

It should have been a peaceful place, but it wasn't. Neil had never felt more uneasy. Fleur's tight, damp grip showed she felt the same.

"No birds." His voice was stifled, stuck in the unmoving air. He wished he hadn't spoken. Their sneakers made no sound on the soft path.

No midges danced around their heads, either. No fly buzzed, no cricket chirped. Neil was almost sure that if he were to get down on hands and knees and part the grass blades, he would find not a single ant or spider.

Nothing lived here except the yew trees and themselves. Nothing made any sound. Except . . . He raised his head. Yes, there it was. Water. Water running somewhere near.

The musical tinkling grew more distinct as they walked the curving path, and the amber of the sky grew richer.

Neil's chest heaved as he took a breath. It wasn't a lack of air, it was excitement tinged with fear. They were approaching a place as highly charged as a power station.

They walked and walked. The curving walls of yew unreeled towards them. Where was the way in?

"This is the inner circle," Fleur muttered. "Shouldn't be taking this long."

"It has to be soon." If there was another illusion in the way . . .

Then, around the curve ahead, a gap appeared in the dark wall to their right. They stopped in front of it. Fleur's hand tightened.

The opening between the two hedges was just wide enough for two people to pass through together. Beyond, there was nothing to see. Just more grass, another hedge.

Nothing there. Why am I scared?

Fleur's hand pulled at his. They stepped through the gap side by side. Then walked out to the middle of the oval space and stood close together, looking around. Swaying slightly, a little dizzy from having walked in circles so long, Neil thought. It looked the same as the false centre, though with no fountain or bench.

It was empty. Silent except for the singing of the invisible brook. Fleur leaned close to Neil and murmured, "It's like nobody's ever been here. Nothing's been here, not even dust. It's like a picture."

Each yew needle gleamed as if polished, each tiny dark blade reflected a sliver of amber sky. The oval of long grass was deep emerald.

"Now what?" Fleur whispered. "My head's spinning."

"Mine too." The dizziness grew worse. As if he stood on a revolving platform at the fair. Neil staggered and suddenly sat down. Fleur fell onto her knees beside him.

The music of the water was louder.

"What's the matter with us?" Fleur asked desperately.

Neil tried closing his eyes, but the spin in his head grew unbearable then, and it set up a matching spin in his stomach. He opened his eyes and fought down a wave of nausea. Try to focus on details, he told himself. Like . . .

"It's wet here." The turf was damp and spongy under his pressing hands. "The spring must be clogged up." He started digging. Fleur knelt beside him and clawed at the ground.

The turf came up easily, in handfuls, with masses of fibrous soil attached. They flung the dripping clods aside and dug out more. Right between Neil's knees, water bubbled up from below and sank again. He backed off.

Fleur wet her hands and smeared the wetness over her face. "Helps," she said. Neil followed her example. The water was icy and it shocked his head clear. But it didn't get rid of that spinning feeling.

"Neil. I think we're actually going around."

He nodded. "Keep digging."

They cleared a round lip of stone, then a basin. The spring rose from the centre of this and bubbled off to the right. They cleared a stone trough about two feet long.

By then the water in the basin had lost its muddy look. It sparkled like cut glass in the golden light. Neil realized how thirsty he was. The water looked so clean, it must be all right to drink. Yet he hesitated, bracing his hands on the ground to steady himself against the unsteadiness of everything around him.

Fleur was staring at the water too. She dipped a finger into the spring and raised a drop to her mouth. Just before it reached her lips she shook her hand and sent the drop flying like a shooting star.

"The spring is the centre," she said, as if she'd just worked that out in her head. "Whatever's going on here, whatever makes the place work, the spring is the most important part."

"Where does it . . . " Neil set his mouth. The spinning was worse. He could feel the planet turning underneath him. Any moment it might whirl him off into space. He dug his fingers into the ground.

More clods came away. More of the stone trough came to light, more of the running stream. Neil scooped it clear, knowing this was what they had to do, not questioning how he knew. Fleur worked across from him.

When the trough was three feet long, it plunged. Neil ripped up a big sheet of turf and exposed a second basin, larger than the first. The babbling of the water burst up at them from here. This was the drain. And it was more.

The water spilled down a spiral of stone steps. They curled down into the darkness, the water gleaming as it slipped over the worn edges. The stairs looked like ice.

"It's the bridge." Fleur's voice came from a distance.

Neil leaned over the pit. Sick, dizzy, his balance gone. He had enough wits left to know this was a place he could never go. Never, into that narrow tube, down into the twisting arms of a stream, into the embrace of the earth.

For Fleur, with her phobia, it would be ten times worse.

"This is the end," he said. "We can't go down there."

"We have to. I'll go first." Fleur's face had gone sharp white. She was already on her way, hands braced on the edge of the pit, feet on the first step.

"But you . . . "

"If I mess up now I'll never have another chance. And we'll never rescue Charlotte. Or Jasper. Or your dad."

Quickly, as if afraid she might change her mind, Fleur swung her feet over the stairs and slid down. Neil hesitated one moment, then climbed down after her.

The steps looked wickedly slick, but his rubber soles clung to the stone. His jeans were drenched at once.

One step down. Another. He splayed his hands on the streaming walls and fought the spinning sensation. Down, down into the dark. He couldn't see Fleur's head below him, but he could hear her loud breathing.

Down and around, water bubbling beneath his feet, swirling around the walls, fountaining over his fingers.

Everything was spinning now. The stairs were a spiral of water boring through earth and darkness. The musical chatter swelled to a roar.

Through his fingertips, Neil felt the moment of change. A flicker in the stone.

Silence.

The spinning grew and grew. Glittering spirals whirled in the hugeness of space. Neil was an atom at the centre of a galaxy, the smallest thing in the universe. He was lost with no chance of ever being found.

Seventeen

There was nothing but darkness and the sound of water flowing. Neil closed his eyes, let them rest a moment, then opened them again. The spinning had stopped. A few feet away, a pale shape stirred. It was Fleur, in her white pants.

"Neil?"

"Right here."

"What is this place?"

"Don't know. Feels like . . . " His hands moved over the ground around him. The grass was gone. "Rock or cement. And here's the edge of the basin where the spring comes up."

"That's not right." Her breathing was loud. She made scuffling noises as she got to her feet. "The spring rose up there. Down here, we should see a stairway."

"Where's *up there*? We're really some place else now. Looks like a cellar. Smells like . . . " He sniffed. Damp and cold, yes, but more like a shore than a house.

"I never liked cellars." She sounded snappish. He didn't snap back. He wasn't feeling any braver than she was, just hiding it differently.

His eyes were used to the dark by now. There was no stairway. Walls, instead of hedges, rose all around. They looked as if they might be made of large, smooth blocks of stone. A faint grey-blue light gave them a pearly sheen.

The same light glinted on the water as it gurgled out of its basin and along a trough. This trough was wider and longer than the one in the maze. It led out through a doorway into even thicker darkness.

"I'm soaked!" Fleur muttered grumpily. "And I'm freezing cold. Where's that wind coming from?"

"There must be windows." His eyes moved up the walls, searching, and then his breath died in his throat. Fleur's fingers gripped his arm and dug in.

"Oh," she said. "Oh . . . my . . . "

They were not in a cellar. No roof hung over their heads. Instead there was a sky crammed with stars. Neil had never seen such a crackling magnificence, such a diamond sharpness.

Fleur stood with her head tilted back and her mouth half open. "Oh, it's beautiful. It's . . . *Neil*."

He was so dazed and dazzled, he didn't hear her.

"Neil!"

"What?"

"Where's the Big Dipper?"

He looked for it, but there was no finding it in that riot of light. Every second or so, a splinter would break loose and streak across the sky, leaving bright arrows on the inside of his eyelids.

"Where's the Swan?" She was getting louder by the second. "I know those shapes, we learned them last year. Where are they? *Neil!*"

"I don't think they're there," he said carefully.

For a moment he couldn't hear her breathing. Then, "I don't think so either," she said. "We're . . . we're awfully far from home, aren't we, Neil?"

"Yes. Awfully far from home."

Panic tugged at him. For a moment he balanced on the brink of an abyss. Then he pulled his gaze from the beautiful and alien stars, and eased himself back from the edge.

"Let's go look for Charlotte."

Fleur took a deep, shaky breath. "Let's."

∽

There was no way out except by wading in the stream. It flowed out the gap and away between straight walls, and it filled the space between, leaving no dry edges for walking.

It felt like the melt-water from snowbanks in March. Before they had gone a dozen steps, their feet were numb and clumsy with cold.

They rounded a corner, and a little way on came to a branching of the path. The stream flowed off to the right. Fleur splashed out onto the dry stone path to the left.

"My feet! I can't even feel them . . . Ow, now I can!" She pulled off her sneakers and shook them, sending water spraying all around.

Neil stood watching the stream. "We're in another maze. A stone one, this time."

"Don't tell me we're lost again!"

"I don't think so. Don't you recognize this spot?"

"Don't play riddles now, Neil, I couldn't stand it." With murderous twists, Fleur wrung water from her shoes.

"We're at the same place where the Uglies caught up to us. Only the path bends the other way, like in a mirror. And everything's straight lines and angles, instead of curves."

"So you know the way out?"

He nodded at the stream. "Follow the water. I've got a hunch . . ."

"Wouldn't you know it." She craned her neck up at the walls. "No chance of walking up there where it's dry? No, too high. Okay." She yanked the sodden sneakers back on. "Let's get this over with."

Neil's hunch proved itself. A few minutes of splashing along the stream bed brought them to a sharp corner they

remembered. At each branching of the way, the stream followed the true path.

"Not exactly original, is it?" Fleur said. Having something
active to do had restored her nerve. "This world of Dexter's,
I mean. He could have created anything — anything brand
new and wonderful. And he made this."

"Looks pretty original to me."

"But it isn't!" She waved an arm angrily as she sloshed on.
"It's taken things from our world and sort of pushed them
out of shape. Or reversed them. Like this maze: you've got
stone instead of leaves, and water instead of turf, and hard
for soft, and cold for warm. Also, dark instead of light. And
it's backwards, even!"

"The stars aren't so bad."

"Yeah, the stars are gorgeous. That's why I can't believe *he*
made them."

They found the entrance at last. Fleur poked about in the
dimness for the stone with the bronze plaque on it, or its
cousin in this world, but didn't find it.

"The land looks different, too," Neil said. "But it's hard
to see. I wish there was a moon."

"Better yet, a sun!"

The starlight on the landscape was only a silver haze over
darkness. All they could be sure of was that from where they
stood at the entrance to the maze, the ground rose. This
maze stood in a valley instead of on a hill.

Neil turned in slow circle, trying to spot some landmark.
Anything that looked familiar. "What else has he changed? If
everything's different, how are we going to find Charlotte?"

"We should look for the house, or something like it."

"That means . . ." Neil thought, then pointed. "Find the
shore, then follow it north. That way we can't get lost."

The stream ran away into the dark through a gully. From
that direction came a long-drawn-out rushing sound, that

grew to a booming, and faded, and swelled again, in a slow rhythm.

Fleur listened, frowning. "Doesn't sound much like . . . " Then she sniffed.

Neil caught it at the same moment."Wood smoke!" A fragrance on the slow breeze, it came from the right, inland. "We should go that way. Maybe we can find somebody to help us!"

"I don't know. It may mean people, but . . . " Her shoulders twitched. Neil knew what she meant. What kind of people?

"Let's find the house," he said.

They followed the stream through the gully. It was hard going. They slipped and climbed among tumbled boulders, trying to stay out of the icy water. In one place the water plunged into a deep pothole, where it swirled and bubbled in a way that reminded Neil of the spiral pit that had brought them to this world.

"D'you suppose . . . " Fleur leaned over the seething hole. "It's the way back? I hope not!"

The stream gushed out of the pothole again and down the gully and finally spilled into the lake. But it was not the same lake they'd known at home.

Waves edged with a coldly glowing white scum heaved higher than their heads, curled and toppled onto the pebbles. Surf tumbled up the beach in a shining froth almost to the gully's mouth.

"It's an ocean!"

Fleur sniffed. "Only the best for Mr. Gunn." She was going to say more, but Neil grabbed her shoulder.

"Listen!"

A voice came to them through the thunder of the surf. Neil stared both ways along the beach. Finally he spotted a dark figure scrambling along the narrow, rocky strip between the bluff and the water. No more than a sketch in the darkness, but Neil knew him instantly.

"Jasper! Over here!" He jumped and waved.

"What's he yelling?" Fleur asked.

"Can't tell."

Jasper waved back as he ran. It was a fierce, downward motion of the arms.

"I think," Fleur said uncertainly, "he's saying *get down.*"

"Why down?" Automatically, Neil looked up.

Above them, in a big inky patch, the stars were gone. He stared, puzzled.

The stink gave them a moment's warning. It rolled over them like a wind from a garbage dump, hot and thick with rottenness. They ducked instinctively, crouching into the smallest space possible between the rocks of the gully. A scream tore their ears.

Then the putrid smell faded. Neil peered up for the stars, found them, and breathed again.

Fleur sat up and raised a trembling hand to her head. One of her gold combs was gone, and her hair was all raked up along one side. A violent shudder ran over her and she curled up into a tight ball.

Neil hovered over her, not sure what to do. A dark figure landed next to him with a slap of rubber soles on rock.

"Fleur? Neil? Are you hurt?"

Fleur jerked her head up. "Neil's fine. And I've still got my scalp. Good thing I'm wearing my good-luck charm!" Her laugh was ragged.

Jasper knelt beside her and put his arms around her. They rocked together for a few minutes, while Neil watched in silent wonder. Where had Jasper learned to do things like that, so naturally?

Abruptly Fleur pushed Jasper away. "You had us worried!" She sounded strong again, accusing and laughing at the same time. "Couldn't you show up in a store window, or phone, or something?"

"I had to stay out of sight for a time, that's all. You should have known it's no easy job to kill a shade."

"But you're not a shade any more, are you?" Neil punched his arm cheerfully. "You feel pretty solid to me."

"In this world, I'm almost real." Jasper's quick smile flashed. "As real as anything can be here."

Fleur looked him over. "Uh-huh. Some bits are still a bit fuzzy. Like, I can't tell exactly what fabric that T-shirt is."

"Never mind, that'll come." Neil gently batted at his twin's ear, and Jasper ducked, laughing. "You're getting realer all the time. And when we go home . . . "

He broke off, astonished at the wave of joy that surged through him. If he were standing it would have lifted him off his feet. Till this moment it hadn't really hit him that his brother would come home, would live with him.

They'd be in the same class at school. At home they'd share a room. Do projects together, listen to music, work out puzzles. Talk in the dark, after lights out. Go everywhere together. Long walks, trips. And Dad —

"Dad!" Neil grabbed his hair. "I don't know how we're going to explain this to him. But wait till he sees you! Can't you just see the look on his face?"

"Yes." Jasper stood up and brushed sand from the knees of his jeans. "But we must move on. There are things you must know before you can rescue Charlotte."

His tone was a dash of cold water in Neil's face. *Why isn't he as excited as I am?* As he followed his twin over the rocks he told himself, *I guess it's just his style. It's how he is.*

༄

They filed along the narrow strip of beach toward the house, or toward where it would have been in their own world. Jasper took the lead. The lake no longer towered and crashed. As if somebody had gotten tired of trying to impress them that way.

Light-edged waves still foamed up the beach, but now they could hear themselves talk without shouting. They could hear other noises, too. As they skirted the base of the bluff, bits of earth pattered down on them. Fleur jumped back as a fist-sized rock bounced past her.

"What's up there?"

"Don't worry," Jasper said casually over his shoulder.

"Don't worry, he says! After that flying whatsit nearly scalped me? What was that thing, anyway?"

"An idea of Dexter's. Meant to frighten you off."

Neil whistled. "You mean, Dexter made that?"

"Of course. He made almost everything in this world. I thought you understood that. What Dexter thinks, becomes . . . not exactly real, but the next thing to it."

"Real enough." Fleur shuddered.

A few yards ahead the path began, a pale ribbon trailing up across the face of the bluff. They still didn't know what was up on that bluff.

Dull thuds came from that direction, a shaking in the earth that Neil felt through his sneaker soles. Flickers of light, like heat lightning, licked up the sky on that side.

"Luckily," Jasper was saying, "there's more at work here than Dexter's mind. Charlotte's been dreaming — "

They had no warning at all. The beast was clever enough to learn from experience: this time it came from downwind. It splashed down in front of them out of nowhere and the spread of its ragged wings darkened the beach. Its stink billowed over them as it lurched to find footing for too many pairs of legs in the shallow water.

"Back!" Jasper yelled, but the other two were already scrambling over the rocks the way they'd come. Only to jostle to

a stop as the beast vaulted over their heads and landed on
the other side of them.

They backed away shoulder to shoulder. The huge sagging
body and leathery wings scraped after them.

"It's clumsy," Neil gasped. "If we all run different dire-
tions — "

"It'll hunt us down one by one," Jasper said. "We can't
outrun it."

Fleur forced a laugh. "Maybe it won't attack. Maybe it'll
just kill us with ugliness."

It had no face. Where the head should have been, a nest
of whitish tentacles twisted like tormented worms. They
glistened in the glow from the surf. Some straggled outward,
others curled into the mouth-hole in the centre of the nest.

In and out, in and out, they never stopped moving. They
looked like octopus tentacles, except that instead of suckers,
they had . . . Neil felt sick.

Hands. Human-looking hands, complete with thumbs.
The ones along the thickest part of the tentacles, nearest the
body, were big and muscular, the backs hairy. The ones nearest
the fine tips of the limbs were small and plump, like babies'
hands.

But all of them had nails that were sharp and caked with
dirt, and all of them snatched at the air as the beast lurched
closer. Jasper caught Fleur's arm on one side and Neil's on
the other and they scrambled.

As they turned, a gleam caught Neil's eye. A twist of gilt
metal clutched in one of the baby hands. Fleur saw it too.

It was insult piled on top of horror. She went crazy. "It's
wrecked my comb!" she screamed. Pulling free, she snatched up
a rock and hurled it. One of the tentacles jerked and hung
twitching.

Jasper bent to the beach, scooped and threw. "Aim for its
mouth!" Neil stooped beside him. Rocks and sand showered

through the air. Tentacles flinched. The beast screeched and hunched down. Fleur laughed with triumph.

Then it clustered its legs and leaped. Not away, but toward them. Tentacles stormed at Neil. Fleur hurled her last rock.

"Neil, get back! Get — "

A dozen hands picked her up as if she weighed nothing at all and aimed her at the eagerly opening mouth.

Eighteen

Fleur wasn't screaming any more. She hung limp in the grip of a dozen hands.

"It's going to eat her!" Neil yelled himself hoarse. He snatched up rocks, hurled them and stooped for more. Some of his stones thudded into the widening O of the mouth, but the beast ignored them.

Then through the uproar of splashing and yelling came a roll of thunder. The beast went rigid. All its tentacles quivered. Neil gaped up at it, and wondered why the thunder hadn't died away, but instead was growing louder.

Then Fleur was sprawling in the water at his feet, and the beast was flapping up into the dark sky, and a stream of horses swept down the path from the bluff.

Sand and foam sprayed, legs and manes flew. The stampede parted around Neil and Jasper as they crouched over Fleur, holding her head out of the water.

Neil caught a glimpse of a large dark eye set in a proud head. Then a milky shoulder with hints of fire and gold deep down, as if the flesh were glass.

The hooves flickered, the sleek backs moved through a haze of light. They glowed from within. Horses made of light.

"They're hers," Jasper shouted in Neil's ear. "Charlotte's!" His smile was radiant.

Fleur pushed against their hands and made an urgent, muffled noise.

"I think," Neil began, "she's going to be . . . "

Jasper held her shoulders while she was sick, then they both gripped her arms and together they staggered to the beach.

Neil would have liked to stay and watch the horses as they played in the surf, kicking up showers of phosphorescence, but Jasper urged him on up the path.

"Is that what you meant?" Neil took a last look back as he climbed. "When you said there are other things at work here besides Dexter's mind?"

"That's right." Jasper paused halfway up the path. He let go of Fleur and she sank onto a rock sticking from the side of the bluff. "Dexter made this world dark, because his mind is dark. It was Charlotte who dreamed the stars."

Fleur's back straightened. "I thought so!"

"And her horses are the enemies of his monsters. She's dreamed other things, too. Birds that used to visit her in great flocks, bringing news from far away. But . . . she doesn't hear them now."

Fleur was starting to look more alive. "Well, the stars are nice, but I'd rather see the sun. And by the way, when is sunrise? Feels like we've been in the dark for months."

"There is no sunrise."

They stared at him. Neil shook off a shudder. "What?"

"You still don't see it, do you?" Jasper smiled at them, but it was a poor effort. "The sun never rises here. Time hasn't begun. That's the worst of it for Charlotte. She's locked up forever. She can't even die."

Neil looked back at the beach. It looked drab now that the horses had drifted on. The lake was a grey shimmer under the stars. Next to it, the land was a pit of black nothing.

Then he looked again. Not nothing. As if the breeze had stirred a branch, a yellow light flickered from the blackness. Then another.

Fleur grabbed his arm. "There *are* people here!"

"Of course there are," Jasper said. "There's quite a large village. And I don't think Dexter put them there. They have names for him . . . " He smiled. "The friendliest is Shadowheart."

"So Charlotte must've dreamed them!"

"But if she's so good at dreaming, why couldn't she dream herself free?" Neil asked.

"Yeah, why didn't she get the people to come rescue her?"

Jasper shook his head. "They did try. Once. They came marching up here with scythes and billhooks."

"And they failed?" Fleur demanded. "You'd think a village could take care of one man!"

"You forget, those people are like me — they're shades. Dexter created this world, so he rules."

Neil waved at the darkness below. "But why would Dexter be satisfied with this — this shadow place? I mean, why doesn't he make himself a real world?"

"Remember what I said about the pattern? How he used it to twist this world out of yours? Then left a piece of it out, he didn't finish it?"

"Yeah. But you didn't explain all that," Fleur said.

"Well, listen now. Since the pattern isn't finished, this world is still attached to your world by the maze. It isn't separate, so it isn't quite real. And in a world of half-real things, a real person has great power. Especially the person who made that world."

"I think I'm getting it," Neil said. "If this world became *really* real, Dexter wouldn't have any more power here than . . . well, than I would in our world."

"That's right. Time would pass, things would change, and be born, and grow and die, in the normal way. Nature would rule. There'd be no more monsters coming out of Dexter's mind."

"Or dream horses out of Charlotte's?" Neil felt a little sad.

"The important thing is this," Jasper said. "His power will be gone. He won't be able to keep her caged up any more."

"So to rescue her, we have to finish the pattern." Neil scratched his leg through his jeans. His wet clothes were chafing. "But how do we do that? We don't even know what this pattern is!"

"You will."

Fleur sighed. "More puzzles."

Jasper smiled and touched her arm, where rows of purplish bruises were starting to show even in the dimness. "Ready?"

She pulled a face. "Ready as I'll ever be, I guess." She got up and stretched. Then froze, with her arms outspread.

Next moment they were down in a knot on the path, huddled as close against the earth as they could get. Neil held his breath. Stuck on the open hillside, there was no way they'd escape the creature this time.

But the stink faded as fast as it had come, and the patch of inky blackness drifted away from them over the beach.

For a moment it was lost between them and the forest. Then a streak of red light darted at the sky from the woods. A scream tore their ears. The inky patch slid towards the lake and was gone.

Neil's legs trembled as he stood.

"You see?" Jasper said. "They have all they can do just to stay alive. They can't help us."

They climbed on up the path. It grew steeper. The last few yards, they used their hands and knees as much as their feet. Neil, coming last, hauled himself up between two boulders at the top and found Jasper and Fleur staring along the height of land.

There was no house. Just a tall, pale grey shaft standing alone on a hillock. It was strangely easy to see in the darkness.

Then Neil saw that it glowed by itself, like the horses. But this was a cold, sickly glow that reminded him of the dead no-colour of a frog's belly.

"Not much like the tower on your house, Neil," Fleur said. There was no green copper dome, no graceful arches.

"All the same it is that tower." Jasper gave it a fierce look. "This is the special place Dexter built for Charlotte. He called it her bower. But here, it's her jail."

The stony hillside was bare of grass. A cold wind whistled among the stones and chilled their bodies under their damp clothes.

Here and there, sharp objects jutted up. Broken blades, wooden poles snapped short. Neil stubbed his toe on something that rang like iron.

They mounted a last steep knoll and halted an arm's length from the tower wall. Instead of separate stones it was all one piece. Its surface was grey and slimy-looking, like slugs crawling over toadstools in damp woods.

"Hey, wait a minute." Neil looked around nervously. "How come we got this near? Why hasn't he stopped us? Where is he?"

Jasper only shrugged. Fleur was too busy searching for the door to listen. "Here it is! Look, it's all made of iron and there's a big bolt on the outside. That proves it's a jail!"

She grasped the ring on the end of the bolt and wrenched at it. For a moment it stuck, then it pulled free so suddenly she fell over.

The door screeched open. A spiral staircase wound upward, the steps and walls putting out that same toadstool glow. Fleur scrambled up off the ground.

"Fleur, wait!" Neil grabbed her arm. "This doesn't feel right."

She pushed his hand away and charged up the stairs two at a time. Neil ran up after her. She didn't stop till she reached the open archway at the top.

Neil caught up with her there. He looked over her shoulder and whistled.

The round room was crammed with carved and polished furniture, all in dark wood and silver and crystal. All coldly glittering.

"It's like a jewel box," she whispered.

"It's crazy," he whispered back.

No colour showed anywhere. Maze patterns in black and white swirled across ceiling, walls and floor.

"It's enough to blind you!" Neil said.

Fleur looked around uneasily. "Where's Charlotte?"

Neil saw, and pointed. Jasper had gone to kneel beside what looked like a short, black pillar near one wall.

The pillar was the back of a tall-backed armchair upholstered in black velvet. Fleur brushed her fingers across the back of the chair and muttered, "Just like cat's fur." The velvet arms curved in snugly across the girl's body, almost meeting in the middle.

The chair faced the one window in the room, an opening a foot tall and six inches wide. Fleur stared at it, then glanced at Neil. Her eyes looked hot. He knew what she meant.

Just big enough to see through. Just enough to make her wish, and dream . . .

Fleur knelt down beside Jasper. "She doesn't know I'm here," he said. "She's gone. She's lost."

Fleur squeezed his hand. "Well, we're here to get her back, aren't we?" But Neil saw her shiver.

Charlotte looked like a life-sized doll. Dark hair cascaded around a pale face and down over the blue silk-covered shoulders. The dress was tight to the waist, where it billowed out into yards of skirt.

Fleur touched a sleeve. "She's so cold. And look at her eyes!"

They were blue as Fleur's, but they stared like glass marbles. Once in a while they closed slowly, then opened again.

Fleur looked across her at Neil. "Now I know why claustrophobia runs in our family. It was her, trying to reach us. Calling for help."

"Okay, let's get her out of there." Neil grabbed at one of the chair arms and yanked. It moved, but the wrong way. It curled tighter around Charlotte's body, sluggish and blind as a worm. He snatched his hands away in horror.

"It's no good," Jasper said.

"And she was just off to see the world," Fleur said. All at once she jumped to her feet and yelled at the walls around her. "Dexter! Where are you? Come on out, you coward!"

Jasper caught her arm. "Don't taunt him!"

She was too furious to listen. "What's the matter, Dexter, you scared to fight a girl? Get out here and I'll tear your head off!"

Silence. She stood sizzling. Neil went and stood beside her. Jasper stayed where he was, crouched beside Charlotte.

Then the marble floor shivered. A ripple passed over the wildly patterned walls, and a soft wind breathed through the room like a sigh. The sigh deepened to a rushing, then a roar. Then a booming, that bounced off the hard surfaces all around them.

Laughter: vast, hollow, pitiless, bellowing up at them from the stone throat of the tower.

Neil crouched down with his hands over his ears. Beside him, Fleur was folded into a ball, with her arms wrapped around her body. The noise was like boulders rolling down on them. Neil could not even begin to deal with the idea that was forming in his brain.

Instinct made him look at the doorway, the way of escape. The moment he looked, it began shrinking. Before he could make a move toward it, it was gone, the wall as smooth as if there never had been a door at all.

Dexter was here, after all. He'd been here all the time.

Dexter was the tower.

Nineteen

The hollow laughter died away. But now that they knew, Dexter's presence was overpowering. Under his feet Neil could feel a rhythmic quiver in the stone floor, and he knew it was Dexter's heartbeat. His breathing came and went in the air that sighed around them.

They were in his hands.

Fleur pushed herself up off the floor. "This doesn't bother me," she announced to nobody in particular. "I'm not scared. I'm not going to be sick."

"Stay calm," Neil told himself loudly. "First thing, we get that door open again. It has to be an illusion, just like that piece of the hedge in the maze, when we . . . "

As he spoke, he walked briskly to where the door had been. He raised a fist and smashed it down on the wall. Then yelled with pain and backed off, nursing a bruised fist under his other arm.

Marching to a nearby bookcase, a fancy thing with ebony pillars crowned by silver eagles and filled with leather-bound books, he tilted his head to read the titles.

"*Utopia*, by Dexter Gunn." He ran a finger along the row of spines. "Would you believe this? Every single book has got his name on it!"

Fleur tried to laugh through chattering teeth.

Neil pulled down an armload of books and fired them at the wall where the door had been, one after the other. They bounced off and crashed to the floor. He raked his hands through his hair.

"I knew this was a trap, I could feel it!" He glared at Fleur.

"Then why did you let us come up here?" she flared. "How dumb could you get?"

"Let you!" His voice went up an octave. "I tried to stop you! You wouldn't listen!"

"Okay! Okay! I messed up. Totally! So, what are we going to do now?"

"I don't know." He kicked at the strewn books.

"Look around," Jasper said softly.

Neil shot him a puzzled look. His twin was standing like a toy soldier beside Charlotte's chair. Jasper's eyes met Neil's, then Fleur's, then strayed toward the centre of the room.

Neil peered around. What did Jasper mean? There was a lot to look at.

Beside the bookcase stood a tall mirror framed by an angel's face, wings and robes, all in silver. There was a chess table with legs carved to look like lions' paws. Nearby loomed an enormous dresser so richly carved that you couldn't tell where the drawers were.

More furniture in the same style stood skewed about the room, in no special order. There was far more of it than one person would ever need.

And clocks were everywhere. Small ones like jewels, and big, dignified ones, including a grandfather clock shaped like a church tower, complete with gargoyles leering from the roof. But all of them stood silent, their hands fixed at twelve. Not one pendulum moved.

Fleur was looking at them too. "If time doesn't move here, why so many clocks?"

"It's another of his jokes," Neil said.

In the middle of the floor was a stone basin about ten feet across, surrounded by a black iron lattice fence. A small hole marked the centre. It looked like a fountain that had gone dry.

"Just a bunch of fancy junk," he announced.

Jasper stared hard at him. "Look *around*."

Around. Behind the furniture, was that what he meant? The crazy patterning of the room itself. A swirling pattern that made Neil think of the maze.

Fleur stood very still. Like Neil, she followed the lines with her eyes.

All over the ceiling and walls, bands of dead black swirled over glowing white. The same pattern continued without a break in the black and white marble floor.

The bands were wide on the ceiling, narrower on the walls and shrank to threads as they spiralled toward the basin in the centre of the floor. All the swirling lines ran into the basin, growing finer and finer till they merged into a glowing mesh.

At the centre of the glow was the small black oval which Neil had thought was the end of a water pipe. He clenched his hands in sudden excitement.

Not a hole after all, at least not for water. It was the size and shape of a fingertip. It was also the size and shape of . . .

Fleur curled her fingers around the oval pendant on her bracelet and hid it in her palm. Neil let out a stifled breath. He shot a glance at Jasper and got a flicker of a smile in return.

Jasper had known all along, of course. He'd had a good reason for keeping that bit of information to himself till now.

Because once the knowledge was in their minds, the Uglies would have felt it. And pounced. The rescue would have been over before it started: they wouldn't even have reached the maze.

Did Dexter know what they'd carried with them into his world? If he did, he didn't seem to be doing anything about it.

"What d'you think?" Fleur asked in a husky voice.

"I think the sooner the better," Neil murmured.

"I think so too."

She stepped to the edge of the basin, grabbed the iron fence, stuck a foot among its curls and swung the other leg up and over. She dropped to a crouch on the inside and started scuttling down the shallow curve on hands, feet and rear end. The black oval was almost within reach, the job was as good as done.

Too easy.

Suddenly Fleur was sliding down a steep slope and trying to stop. Invisible hands gripped the basin from below and pulled it into a deep, narrow shaft. The marble stretched like rubber, yet it was still too smooth and hard for her to grip.

She saved herself by jamming feet and back against the sides of the shaft. Neil was hanging over the iron railing by then, straining to reach her. The basin was now a glowing tube plunging to a speck of black, miles below.

"Hurry!" Fleur screamed. "Get me a rope — anything!"

Neil stared around wildly for a rope, pawed at his T-shirt — useless — then thought of getting a pendulum out of one of the bigger clocks.

"*Neil!*"

The floor above her head was shrinking together. For a moment Neil saw her face through an opening the size of a dinner plate. Then it was the size of a dime, then it was gone. The basin was sealed off, and Fleur was walled up alive.

♋

Neil was over the fence in one jump and scrabbling at the stone floor. "Let her out!" he yelled. "Dexter! Let her out of there!"

Immense laughter boomed around him. When the echoes died, he found himself looking at Jasper through the iron fence.

"Calm yourself," Jasper said. "You can't do it that way."

"We can't leave her in there! Not with her phobia."

"I know. Use your mind."

"What are you talking about?"

"Dexter does things with his mind, so . . . "

Neil clenched his fists. "I'm only human."

"So is he. You're just like him — just as real. More real than the stuff this tower is made of. You can do what he can. That is, if you really want to."

There was a faint jeer in the last few words. It started Neil simmering. "Don't compare me to him!"

"Why not? Can you deny it?" Jasper's silver eyes were cold. "It's always Neil at the centre of your world, isn't it? You've already forgotten about Fleur."

Coming from Jasper, it was a slap in the face.

"No!" Neil shoved furiously at the floor and shot to his feet.

Then nearly toppled over with shock. He bent down, peered at the floor. Stared at his hands. Jasper grinned.

Neil crouched down again and fitted eight fingers and two thumbs into the ten small dents in the floor in front of him. He looked at his hands again, then at Jasper.

"You said those things just to get me going, right?"

Jasper chuckled. "You did get fired up!" Then his smile faded. "But if anger is what you need, there are better ways to find it. Think of Charlotte."

Neil nodded. But at once his thoughts went to Fleur. Shut in there with her worst nightmare.

"I'll bet Dexter's getting a great kick out of it, too," he muttered.

She might be raving with panic by now. She might have fallen to the bottom of that miles-deep pit. She could be lying dead . . .

Neil took a deep breath. It had always been his way to put a lid on anger. You stayed cool, calm and in control, that was the way his dad had raised him.

Dad. Lying in a hospital bed, with eyes as dead and blank as Charlotte's.

A deep fury rose up in him. He let it come. For a moment it scared him, for this was no hot emotion but a hard, cold thing like a steel blade. If there'd been time he would have choked it down.

But there was no time, and no choice. It welled up and filled him. His fingers dug into the stone. He ripped out a chunk as if it was raw clay and shouted through the hole he had made.

"Fleur! You okay?"

"No! Hurry up!"

Her voice sounded strained and muffled, but strong. He caught a glimpse of her about three yards below.

"Hold on!" he yelled. "I'll get you out!"

"No! Just give me a rope, or something. I want to go down!"

"But I can't get at you!" In frustration he tore up more of the floor. Sweat dripped from his forehead. It was harder now. His strength was seeping away.

"Your mind," Jasper said, from behind him. "Use your mind, not your muscles!"

"My mind. But how do I . . . " He closed his eyes, wet his dry lips, and concentrated. He pictured the bottom of the basin, a glowing saucer with a black oval at its centre. He saw his hands grown huge on the end of long, long, brawny arms, his fingers linked beneath the basin.

He pulled. Nothing happened. He flexed his shoulders, dug in his heels and pulled with every ounce of . . .

The tower rocked. Fleur yelled.

"Gently!" Jasper said.

Neil opened his eyes and looked down into the hole. The bottom was a few yards closer than it had been. Its brightness glistened on Fleur's face. She was splayed like a starfish, arms and legs all stuck out in different directions.

"You still okay?" he asked.

"A bit . . . less . . . sudden . . . next time. *Please*."

He laughed wildly. "I did it! I shaped the stone! I can shape this place the same way *he* can!"

"Great," Fleur said through gritted teeth.

"Just watch. I'll flatten the well like a pancake!" He reached again with his mind and felt himself growing huge, the well small in his giant hands.

A fierce joy burst through his veins. He could control his strength now. He began to force the stone tube smoothly, slowly back toward its original basin shape.

And when I've got this fixed, he thought, I'll knock the tower down. Then I'll take this world away from Dexter and make it better. I'll give it a sun and a moon and ships and cities and . . . and everything!

Scenes of triumph paraded through his mind as the bottom of the well telescoped toward him. He was distantly aware of Fleur yelling in alarm. The sides took on a wider cone shape, then a deep basin shape . . .

And then it all went hard and lifeless.

Neil stood up, confused. "Jasper? What's going on?"

Jasper was still kneeling outside the fence. He didn't blink. Cold in the pit of his stomach, Neil vaulted over the fence and grabbed Jasper's shoulder. He rocked stiffly, like a statue loose on its pedestal.

"Jasper!"

"Oh, he's quite unharmed, I promise you."

Neil jumped up, turned and backed away. A tall man was stepping out from the mirror with the angel frame.

He had wondered at the no-colour scheme of the room, all the crystal and ebony and precious metal. Now he knew the reason.

Black clothes, tightly buttoned up, with linen edges so white, they shone. A glint of gold chain across the waistcoat. Dark hair, with a sheen to it. A face as smooth and pale as an ivory mask.

Only the eyes looked alive.

Twenty

Dexter strolled forward, looking him up and down. "Well, nephew. You have impressed me, I will say that." His voice was deep and musical, a pleasure to listen to.

Neil pointed at Jasper. "What have you done to him?"

"You may set your mind at ease. The shade and the girl are merely stopped, for the moment. This is truce, nephew." He held up two long hands. "Shall we talk terms?"

Neil backed off warily. After thinking of Dexter for so long as a distant evil, a dark cloud lurking somewhere in the past, it was a shock to see him real and up close.

He was much too solid. His nostrils quivered when he drew breath. Black hairs grew on the backs of his hands, which looked strong despite their slender length. And his eyes had a nasty way of sucking at your face.

"Well, nephew?" He sounded amused, though his mouth never smiled.

"Just let Charlotte go free. That's all we want."

"Oh, no. That's not open to discussion."

"But that's crazy! She's not even *here!*"

"She'll come back. One day she will turn to me of her own accord." His lips bent slightly. "I have all the time in the world."

"Look." Neil knew it was useless, but he had to try reason. "Why don't you think of what *she* wants, for once?"

"It's you that concerns me now, my lad. I suspect you're quite unaware of your danger."

Neil managed a disdainful laugh. "Danger? You're talking garbage!" He circled the fence, to put the basin between them. He didn't like being within Dexter's reach.

Dexter hardly seemed interested. He sauntered about among the furniture, touching a knob here, a corner there. "Have you thought how you're going to get home, once the bridge is gone?"

"Gone?" Neil stood still. "What are you talking about?"

"I mean . . . " Dexter touched a polished shoe to the books scattered on the floor. "I mean, there is only one way this world can become fully real, which I gather is what Jasper wants. To become real, it must separate from the old world."

Neil didn't see the point. "So?"

"So the bridge between the worlds must break." Dexter paused a moment to let that sink in, then added, "You see, Neil, if you complete my pattern, there will be no way home. You'll be trapped here."

"But Jasper didn't . . . " His throat dried up.

"Didn't tell you? Well, he wouldn't, would he?" Dexter shrugged. "Too much chance you'd stop short of what he wants."

"But he wouldn't hold out on me like that! He's my twin brother, my — "

"Your other half?" Dexter's eyes glistened. "You still think he'll go home with you when all this is over?"

"Yes. He promised."

"Then you're a fool! He used that promise to lure you here, to help him steal Charlotte from me. He has not the slightest intention of keeping it."

"I don't believe you!" Neil backed away.

"Nonsense, you've always suspected it! All he cares about is Charlotte."

Neil took an angry breath, but found no words. He couldn't deny this, it rang too true.

Fleur had said it: he'd do anything for Charlotte. *I should have seen it too. I just didn't want to know.*

Dexter was watching him across the width of the basin. The sad mask of his face looked sympathetic. "You thought you were first with him, didn't you? Now you find you're hardly a close second. I know how that hurts."

He does know! Neil was dully surprised.

"Yes." The wide mouth twisted bitterly. "You see, there's a man in here behind the monster you've built up. A man who thinks and feels as you do."

That made sense. In fact, most of what Dexter said made surprisingly good sense.

Neil rubbed his forehead. Nothing was clear any more. When he'd started on this rescue mission it had looked simple, though not easy. Solve the maze, bring Charlotte home, live happily ever after with Dad and Jasper.

Nothing had turned out the way it was supposed to.

"If you really want to keep the shade with you," Dexter said in his musical voice, "I can offer you a way."

Neil blinked at him, confused. They stood only a few feet apart, now. Dexter had moved when he wasn't looking. Alarm prickled up Neil's neck.

"I mean, boy, the power to shape this world is in my hands. And Jasper is made of the stuff of this world. We can force him to be a part of us, if that will make you happy. We'll never be lonely again."

For a moment Neil wavered. Then he heard what the man was really saying. *Force* Jasper? "That's sick! I wouldn't want to force Jasper to do anything!"

"Don't give me that sentimental trash!" A flash of rage cracked the mask, but only for a moment. "It's exactly what you want and you know it!"

"But I —"

"And don't pretend otherwise. The shade belongs to us, he exists only because of us. So he must do as he's told. At least you'll have an easier time than I had with Charlotte."

"No! I'm not like you!"

"You are exactly like me! It's the only reason you've lasted so long against me." Dexter looked over the fence at the jagged hole in the marble floor. "That was destructive. But you enjoyed it, didn't you?"

"I was rescuing Fleur," Neil said feebly. But he remembered what he'd felt as he forced the stone to obey his will. Joy and excitement, yes. And something darker. Now he felt queasy.

Dexter laughed softly. The sound set Neil's teeth on edge. "Face it, lad. Jasper's not your other half. I am!"

No. But Neil could only mouth it. He was too afraid it should be *yes*.

"You forgot about Fleur rather quickly, I think. Oh, I don't condemn you! You and I, we were both born to shape worlds. We were born to rule."

Neil thought of the monster on the beach, and the way it had nearly eaten Fleur. He remembered the Uglies' eyes. "I wouldn't want to rule a stinkhole like this!"

"Then let us change it!" Dexter waved impatiently. "Think, boy! How often have you been offered a world? It doesn't happen every day, does it? We can make this world exactly as we — "

"No." It came out loud and flat and stupid-sounding, but Neil let it stand. He felt as if he'd washed a week's sleep from his eyes. *What got into me?* he wondered.

Dexter's nostrils flared. "You disappoint me. Very well!" He flapped a hand. "Run off home, like the child you are. Stop annoying the grown-ups."

"No, I won't do that either." Neil started back toward Jasper.

"Don't you fear being trapped here?"

He must be afraid, Neil thought. *Why else would he be talking? He's stalling!*

"Well, boy? Do we have a bargain?"

Neil laughed. "What's this *we*? You've never shared anything, you're as selfish as they come!"

"Then we're two of a kind!"

"Oh, no, we're not!" He knelt by Jasper and gripped his shoulder. It was stiff as styrofoam. He dug his fingers in, willing life and warmth back into the hard flesh.

Dexter said nothing. Neil didn't look up till he heard a loud crack, and then a whistle close to his ear. A shining object bounced off the floor nearby. It was one of the gilt eagles from the top of the bookcase.

It rolled to a stop. And then, while Neil stared, it lurched to its feet, wings and claws scraping. The head turned. One glass eye glittered at him. The bird bobbed up and down with a creak-creak of metal joints.

Neil started to laugh. Then ducked as the eagle sprang at him again. It whizzed past him and hit the dresser, gouging a hole in the wood. This time one wing broke off, and it lay still.

He straightened up, gaping. Dexter stood near the bookcase wearing his first real smile.

A second crack, and a third, and a fourth. The other three eagles broke free of their ebony pillars, spread their wings and torpedoed at Neil. He saved himself by diving under the dresser.

Then realized the danger and squirmed out again. Just in time. The wooden legs bent and the dresser sat down like an elephant on the place where Neil had been a moment before.

He jumped up, grabbed a crystal shepherdess from the top of the dresser and flung it. His aim was good, but the figurine veered to one side when Dexter casually raised a hand.

"Save your energy, boy. You can't win, not here."

Neil was too busy to talk. Stay away from large pieces of furniture, he told himself. Watch out for anything small enough to be thrown.

As he crouched near the fence, he noticed Jasper was nowhere in sight. He must have taken cover. So, he was no longer "stopped." One less worry.

Dexter was standing a few feet away from the grandfather clock. One good shove . . .

Neil stared at it. It wobbled. He held his breath and willed, and willed, till he felt himself going red.

Dexter strolled toward him. His eyes shone with amusement. "Oh, Neil. Give it up!"

Push . . . push . . . The clock suddenly leaped up, crashed into the ceiling and showered Dexter with debris. The pendulum clanged as it struck his shoulder.

Dexter stopped smiling. "Blockhead!" He waved at the bookcase behind him. The volumes exploded from the shelves. Neil kept his head down and heard them clang against the fence.

And then something hard and cold circled his neck.

He grabbed at it: a band of metal. It tightened, cutting into his windpipe and choking him. The fence, with its iron curlicues.

His vision swam. He pulled strength back into his fingers and willed it outward. The iron curl sprang open.

He rolled away, and came up against the chess table with lions' paws for feet. They began dancing up and down, trampling him. The heavy chessmen hopped and fell. Neil yelled, but the pain helped. He locked the table in place with a furious thought.

Dexter was still meandering toward him, casual and confident. Neil looked at the table. *Get him!* It pawed at the floor in its eagerness to be off. But all four feet faced different ways, and the table could only dance a frantic jig on the spot.

He gave up on the table and jerked his chin at the chessmen. *Go!* They flew at Dexter like giant hailstones.

Dexter raised his hands, with the fingers together in a steeple shape. The shower parted around him and bounced off the floor. The noise was deafening. He lowered his hands and showed his teeth in triumph.

"All right," Neil said sulkily. He slumped. "You win."

"Not a bad try. Not bad at — "

The table leaped and aimed a kick at Dexter's head. He crumpled to his knees.

"Got him!" Laughing, Neil sprang to his feet and ran toward the fence. Jasper was already inside, scraping helplessly at the hole in the floor. Time to finish the job. Fast!

He forgot to watch his back.

Hands grabbed the waistband of his jeans on both sides and lifted him off his feet. He had a fraction of a second to realize it was the mirror with the angel frame.

It had walked up behind him on its short silver legs. The silver hands held him dangling off the floor and rushed him toward Dexter.

He was as helpless as a puppet on strings. Taken by surprise, he forgot how to concentrate.

Dexter was laughing now, his handsome face twisting till he looked like one of the Uglies. "Now you know why I let you come so far. It's time our two halves became one, don't you think? You'll be my shade, and keep me company . . . forever."

"But you can't . . . I won't . . . "

"I rule here! You'll *be* and *do* as I wish!" He spread out his arms and crooked his fingers, still laughing. "Come on, boy! I can use a clever shade like you!"

The space between them shrank like an elastic band. Neil tried to collapse, to slip to the floor, but the silver fingers gripped his waistband too tightly.

"No!" He leaned back, he dug his heels in, but it did no good. He was dragged yelling and flailing across the floor.

"Use your mind!" someone shouted. But his mind was too jostled. He couldn't focus.

He had two seconds to save himself. Or the next time he looked, it would be from Dexter's skull, through Dexter's eyes. And Neil would no longer exist.

Twenty One

Dexter's face flew at him. Then some shred of battle wit he never knew he had, shouted: *Use that speed!*

In the last split second Neil's fist flashed up. The impact jarred his arm to the shoulder.

He stumbled into a suddenly empty space and fell sprawling. As he sat up, rubbing his shoulder and wincing at the sting in his knuckles, he started laughing.

In the end, the war of minds had come down to fists. He could imagine how Dexter's chin must feel.

"Neil! Hurry!" Jasper yelled. "Before he recovers!"

As Neil scrambled over the fence, the hole he'd made started shrinking again. Fleur yelled. He threw himself down and slid feet-first into the hole with her.

The glowing sides of the pit dropped again, till they were falling through a blur of light.

But this time Neil knew what to do. He called the walls toward him, gently, till he was sliding again. Friction against marble heated the seat of his pants. His heels dug in and squealed and he smelled hot rubber.

The bottom of the tube rushed up at him.

It was a few moments before he realized he was lying on his back, and he'd stopped moving. He scrambled to his knees. Fleur sat up, rubbing her arms and legs.

"One more second." She spaced her words carefully. "And you'd have been picking up little pieces of me."

The glowing basin spread around them, shallow as it had been the first time they'd seen it. The black oval lay within a few inches of Fleur's feet.

"Hurry!" Jasper breathed, from the other side of the iron fence. "Do it now!"

Fleur slipped the chain from her wrist and twisted the pendant off. She crawled across the basin. The marble quivered under Neil's hands, as if straining to explode.

She crouched beside the blank space and laid the pendant on it. A perfect fit. Then sat back and watched. Neil held his breath.

Nothing happened.

"Something's wrong!" he muttered.

"Maybe we made a mistake. Maybe this isn't the right piece after all." Fleur stood up and stretched, grimacing.

Neil smacked the floor in frustration. "We'll have to go back and start all over again!"

Aching and weary in every bone, he pushed up off his knees.

Things began to happen.

The oval piece at the centre flared. It grew brighter and brighter till it stood out white-hot against the pearly glow of the basin.

Neil shielded his eyes. Fleur took a step back. It looked dangerous.

Then came a breathless moment. An instant of total stillness that stretched out and out like a final heartbeat . . .

And snapped. The floor shuddered. Fleur lost her balance and fell. At the same time the glow faded from the basin, leaving it plain, unmarked stone.

"You've done it!" Jasper crowed. "You've finished the pattern!"

Everything was changed. Neil could feel it, hear it, smell it. Fleur jumped into the air and whooped. Then she hugged Neil.

"We did it! We won! We . . . "

The floor shuddered again and she sat down hard.

"I thought it was all over." Neil looked around nervously.

Jasper leaned over the fence and waved at them. "Get out of there!" he yelled. "Now!"

Scared without knowing why, Neil threw himself at the top of the basin and hauled himself up. Fleur scrambled up ahead of him. The stone lip crumbled under her shoes like damp plaster. Neil slid down again.

Then the iron fence clanged flat in a shower of rust. Fleur and Jasper knelt above him, reaching over. He caught their hands and crawled out, just as the basin collapsed behind him. Dust billowed out of the pit.

"What's going on?" he screamed over the noise.

"Dexter's falling apart!" Jasper yelled joyfully. He was already at the black velvet chair, yanking at the arms that held Charlotte prisoner. They cracked off and he tossed them aside.

"Charlotte!" Jasper shook her. She flopped as if she had no bones.

"We'll carry her," Neil said. He got his hands under her armpits while Jasper grabbed her about the knees.

"But if we're sealed in . . . " Fleur looked around. The door was in place again, but now it was just a gap in a wall of rough stones. The black and white pattern had faded from the walls, floor and ceiling.

The walls didn't look too solid, either. Mortar dust trickled from between the stones. The small window became a huge hole as the wall above it collapsed. A breeze swirled the clouds of dust and Neil caught the fishy, watery smell of the lake.

They scuttled awkwardly with their burden through the doorway and lurched down the stairs. Once they had to lift Charlotte across a gap where two steps had fallen in. Fleur scrambled after them, helping where she could: Charlotte was surprisingly heavy.

Neil knew his miraculous strength was gone, because he'd tried to use it. He had no time to wonder if he was sorry or glad.

The whole tower was quaking. The air was so white with dust, any movement was like swimming through milk. They choked and coughed, and tried to hold their breath.

Their luck held. They reached the door at the base of the tower and crunched out over piles of broken stone.

Jasper was still shouting, "Hurry! Hurry!" Fleur grabbed Charlotte by the waist and they staggered down the knoll to the open ground below.

The tower groaned. They cowered, shielding their heads, as the shaft tilted, toppled and fell sideways with a strange slowness. The ground thundered.

♋

"Well," Fleur said, when the ground had stopped shaking and the dust had settled. "We did it! Now we can go home!"

"Can we?" Neil asked. "Can we, Jasper?"

Jasper sat crosslegged on the stony ground, with Charlotte propped in his arms. She was still asleep. He looked across her at Neil.

"I know what Dexter said. I could hear."

"And? Was it true?" Neil held his breath. *Say no!*

Jasper's eyes slid aside. So that was his answer.

"What?" Fleur demanded. "What's going on?"

"We're trapped," Neil said savagely. "Because Jasper didn't tell us the bridge would break when you put that last piece in."

"You mean . . . " Fleur stared at him, then at Jasper. Her voice rose. "We're stuck here?"

"No!" Jasper's head went up. "Why should Neil take Dexter's word, instead of mine?"

"Because I found out you've been lying to me."

"But it hasn't broken yet! See: I belong to this place." Jasper grabbed a rock from beside him and squeezed it in his fist. "I can feel it. The bridge was the first part he made. And it's been touching your world so long, it's always been more real than the rest. It won't be easy to break."

"You're sure of that?" Fleur jumped to her feet.

"I . . . well," he said carefully, "I'm *almost* certain. I was relying on it."

It didn't change things for Neil. "You were never that sure. It was a risk — for Fleur and me. And you didn't tell us."

"It would have been too hard to explain. Remember how I was trying to talk through sugar, and mirrors . . . " He tossed the rock away. "Yes, then! I was afraid I'd lose you, if I told the truth. You were my only hope."

Neil couldn't talk any more. He hurt as if he'd been chopped in half.

"I'll make it up to you, I swear it."

Neil didn't look at him. He didn't believe him.

"We'd better get moving." Fleur stooped to peer into Charlotte's face. "We'll have to carry her again."

At that moment Charlotte opened her eyes. She blinked and rubbed her forehead. Jasper hugged her. She caught sight of his face and laughed.

"Jasper!"

"Welcome back." He smiled down at her in a way that hurt Neil all over again.

She reached up and touched Jasper's chin. "You're not a shade any more! You're real!" Then she caught sight of Fleur.

She sat up and pointed. "I know who you are. I dreamed you!"

Fleur grabbed her hands and gave them a squeeze. "I dreamed you too, sort of. I'm your great-great . . . " She screwed up her face. "Never mind. Just say we're related. Only, it's been a few years."

"Those clothes of yours!" Charlotte fingered the cuff of Fleur's white pants, now more grey than white. Her eyes were wide. "How many years?"

"A hundred and forty-five."

Charlotte's hands flew to her head. "Am I still dreaming?"

"We have to move," Neil said roughly. He couldn't seem to speak any other way. Charlotte scrambled to her feet, with Jasper hovering at her elbow. She caught sight of Neil's face and her eyes widened again.

Fleur looked past her. "Oh-oh. Look out!"

The ruined tower was a ridge of broken stone capping the knoll above them, a lumpy black outline against a pale grey sky. Here and there a table leg stuck up, or an angel's wing. The unhealthy glow of the stones had long since faded.

Something was moving in the ruin. A chunk of stone slid, a figure crawled from underneath it, all rags and elbows. Like a huge insect, crushed but still twitching.

It wavered to its feet and tottered down the knoll toward them. Jasper stepped out in front of Charlotte: she pulled him back. Her face was like white marble.

Dexter stopped a few feet away and held out his hands. For a sickening moment, Neil thought the man was going to cry. The most horrible thing was, now that he'd lost that hard polish, he looked more like Gregory than ever.

"I . . . you . . . " His musical voice was now a croak. He looked at Charlotte, then at Neil. Neil wondered if he was going to beg forgiveness or curse them all. They never found out.

A distant howl drifted to them on the wind. It came from the direction of the beach. Dexter quivered. A second howl rose over the first, and then a chorus broke out. The sound was louder now.

His hands clenched. He hunched. Then he turned and ran away from the howling, inland. He skidded and fell, then picked himself up and disappeared over a hillock.

"D'you think," Fleur said nervously, "we'd better . . . "

Dark shapes vaulted over the ruin and swarmed down the slope toward them.

Jasper's arm went around Charlotte, his other hand grabbed Neil's. "Stand still!"

The pack passed by, yowling and yipping and squealing. The Uglies were all beast now, no trace left of their human disguises. Sharp snouts nosed the trail, clawed feet scattered dirt as they loped along. A pair of yellow eyes flashed at the huddled four. Then the hunt was past. The howling dwindled.

"They'll make hamburger out of him!" Neil said.

Fleur shook herself. "I almost feel sorry for him."

"Don't. He has a few tricks left." Jasper tugged at Charlotte's arm. "Almost time to go."

She didn't answer. She was biting her lower lip and looking around at the barren hillside and the pale sky. Suddenly she grabbed up her skirts in both hands and started running up the knoll. The other three ran after her.

As Neil climbed through the ruin of the tower, he noticed it was getting easier to see. Some of Dexter's books lay wedged between stones. One was pressed open and he saw there was nothing on the pages. Had the print faded, or had they always been blank?

A small round clock, with a sun and moon painted on its face, lay upside down in the rubble. It was ticking steadily. He picked it up and set it on a rock. The hands pointed to 12:30. His own watch said 3:10.

So time had begun. Maybe it was already too late to go back.

They scrambled through the ruin and reached the edge of the bluff beyond. Charlotte grabbed Jasper's arm. "Look!"

Neil squinted over the lake. Across the water, in the place where the horizon would have been if it were visible, stretched a fiery red crack. It grew longer, wider, brighter. It grew too fierce to look at.

"What is that?" Fleur blinked from under her hand. "It looks like the crack of doom."

Then she looked at Neil, and he felt the blood leave his face. The crack of doom.

"We . . . " he faltered. "We brought Dexter down. And he was the creator, so . . . "

"So we've wrecked his world as well. Only, we're still trapped here."

Jasper was saying something, but Neil hardly heard him. He couldn't take his eyes from the fiery crack that was splitting the world in half.

This was it.

After all their work and scheming and puzzling their way through the maze, after escaping death half a dozen times, after beating Dexter and setting Charlotte free — this was the way it was to end.

Twenty Two

It's not fair!" Fleur wailed. "After all the trouble we went to!"

Charlotte threw back her head and laughed. "You ninnies!"

And then Neil understood. Nothing was ending. This was a beginning. It was an event so ordinary yet so wonderful that he'd forgotten it was possible. They'd been in the dark too long.

"It's the sun!" He laughed. "The sun is rising!"

"But . . . isn't that west?" Fleur pointed at the lake.

"Here it's the east." Jasper chuckled. "We're backward here, remember?"

"All of you must do as you please," Charlotte said, "but I'm staying." She shaded her eyes against the glare.

"Staying!" Jasper looked horrified. "But you can't!"

"Why not? I can't go back to my own time, that road is closed. And I'm not sure the future is the right place for me."

"But . . . what about the monsters?"

"And," Neil put in, "what about Dexter?"

"Serpents in the garden." Charlotte shook back her long dark hair, and smiled. "But don't forget, I've been dreaming too. Who knows what may be out there?"

"I'm beginning to see what you mean," Fleur said.

Day was breaking across the land. The more they saw of it, the less it looked like the world they'd left behind. Neil didn't recall a chain of mountains anywhere near Amstey, but they existed here, miles to the north — or was it south? Dark forests lapped up their lower slopes, and their peaks were lost in a golden mist.

The other end of the shore dwindled to rolling hills, soft greens fading to blue and then distant violet. Something shiny winked back at the sunrise from among those hills. Neil wondered what it could be. A window, an enormous gem, a tower of glass?

Far out on the ocean-lake, a sleek grey back the size of an island rose, spouted and sank.

"And it's all ours to discover," Charlotte said happily.

"Oh, I wish, I wish . . . " Fleur whispered.

Neil took a deep breath. The air smelled of clover and pine resin, and other scents that were strange to him. The warmth of a world's first sunrise was on his face. And the four of them were on their own. Free.

Even as he stared, and marvelled, and itched to be out there exploring, he knew it was no good.

"I can't," he said. "There's Dad. He'd think I was dead."

"My folks would think the same." Fleur sighed. "And I've got to confess it: I'd miss Piglet."

"Charlotte?" Jasper sounded tense.

She shook her head firmly. "This world is the only choice for me. I just wish my clothes were more sensible, more like yours, Fleur. This dress isn't made for traipsing through woods."

She plucked at the skirt, then looked at Fleur. "I wonder. Would you consider? . . . "

"A trade? My dirty old pants and shirt for that beautiful dress?" Fleur didn't hesitate. "Come on. But we'd better be quick."

Jasper watched them pick their way behind the ruin of the tower. Then he looked at Neil. "I'm ready to keep my word."

Neil studied him. It seemed to him he'd never looked at Jasper as an actual person before, only as a copy of himself.

"You don't want to go back with me. So don't say you do. Besides, you can't."

"So you worked that out, too?" Jasper sounded sad. "You're right, I can't go back with you as a real person. Only as a shade, as part of you. It's only here, in this world, I'm real."

"So that's the end of it." Neil turned away. Jasper caught him by the arm.

"I said I'd make it worth your while, didn't I? I promised. And you kept your side of the bargain, you set Charlotte free."

"Forget it."

"Oh, no. No matter what you may think, I never meant to trick you. I'll keep my promise."

Neil said nothing.

"You've waited long enough. You've been missing your other half almost all your life. So, here I am."

Jasper held out his arms. Neil took a deep breath. Then took a step and reached out.

It was like stepping into a mirror and embracing his own reflection. He closed his arms, hugging his brother close, closer. Then only one boy stood on the bluff with his arms clasped across his chest. Jasper was gone.

For as long as it took to draw a breath. And then Neil knew.

Next moment he opened his arms and pushed, and there was Jasper, stumbling backwards. Neil caught him by the arm before he could fall.

Jasper shook his head. "But you need me! How will you get along without me?"

"I've got Dad. We'll do okay."

"But — "

"Look, I'm not like Dexter! I don't put people in jail. Besides, you're not really my other half, are you?"

"Well, um . . . no." Jasper looked apologetic. "I'm just myself."

"Right. I know that now. I knew it as soon as you were there, inside. Taking you back as part of me would be as bad as what Dexter did to Charlotte."

Fleur stepped carefully out of the ruins just then, lifting her new dress over the dusty stones. Charlotte came striding ahead of her in Fleur's white pants and turquoise shirt.

"I feel so free!" she said, and ran the rest of the way to show how easily she could move.

She slipped her arm through Jasper's. "Well, are you staying? Say you will!"

"I . . . " He gazed back and forth from her to Neil. He looked confused and miserable.

"Go on!" Neil said. "It's what you want, admit it. To stay with her. Besides . . . " He punched him gently on the arm. "You're solid now. You can't give that up!"

Jasper squared his shoulders and flashed his brilliant smile. "I'll never forget. We'll always — " He broke off. "Oh, no! Time!"

Neil didn't ask time for what. Without another word they all linked hands and ran. Fleur was on one end of the line, because she had to hold up her skirts with one hand, to keep from tripping. Neil was on the other end.

They stampeded along the edge of the bluff toward the gully, where the stream flowed from the maze. Faster and faster, leaping over rocks, skidding where new grass was fuzzing out of the stony soil like hair on a baby's head.

"We'll break our necks!" Fleur shrieked, between leaps. The slope dropped away, suddenly steep, and the gully opened like jaws below them.

The stream had dried up. The rocks, half buried in mud and slimy with weed, glistened twenty feet below.

They pulled to a halt on the brink. "Too late," Neil panted.

Directly below lay the pothole. It wasn't bubbling any more. Deep in its core lay a dark pool with a spiral of foam spinning at its centre. Hardly any water at all. And as they watched, it gurgled away into the depths of the earth.

"Jump!" Jasper yelled.

"No!" Neil yelled. "We'll be ki — "

Jasper slipped behind him and pushed. The last sounds he heard were *Goodbye, goodbye*, and somebody screaming.

♋

Terror in mid-air. Rocks smashing up at him. Rocks blurring past him. The blur twisting, and Neil twisting with it. His bones were a jelly, his flesh a puff of wind. He was a cloth wrung out to dry.

And then a merciful darkness.

♋

The sun was hot on Neil's cheek. He blinked up at it, puzzled to see it so high in the sky. It was a different sky, too: not the washed pastel of morning but a rich, hazy blue. The sky of an August afternoon.

Grass blades prickled his palms as he sat up. A green wall curved around him, and the air smelled of dust and the lake. He was back in the centre of the maze.

Home. And alive!

The tower, Charlotte, Jasper, that amazing sunrise, they all burned in his mind for a moment. Then, as he groped for the details, they slipped away. He couldn't picture the exact colour of those mountains.

A dream, that's all it was. Yet Neil ached as if he'd lost his home, his best friend. Real treasures.

Then he heard a rustling sound behind him. He looked around and saw Fleur brushing dust from the hem of a long blue silk dress.

"At least we didn't get wet this time," she said.

He pinched a fold of the silk. "It's real!"

"Well, of course it's real. And how I'm going to explain it, I don't know! I mean, an antique dress that's brand new?"

Behind her lay the basin of the fountain, and its trough. They were dry. Neil crawled over to look at the spiral stairs where the spring had run down, and found a damp hole, choked with dirt and stones. He wondered . . .

"Wouldn't work," Fleur said. "I thought of that too. You could dig all the way to Australia. The bridge is gone."

Gone. Ended. Forever.

Neil sat on the grass, hugging his knees. "I'm going to miss him."

Fleur crouched beside him, careless of grass stains on her precious dress. "But you set him free."

"Yeah." He laughed suddenly. "Think of it! Jasper's off to explore a whole new world. He'll have the time of his life!"

♋

The centre of the maze had lost that unnatural hush. Along with the amber light and the stillness, the power was gone. Neil wasn't surprised when they came to the bend where the Uglies had trapped them, and found the way open. Shreds of what might have been a notebook littered the path.

"And you know what?" Fleur was lilting as she walked, swirling her skirts to make the silk shimmer. "I think my phobia's gone. I don't even feel a twinge!"

"I guess it happened when Charlotte came out of that chair. You know, the two worlds were pretty close, in some ways. I wonder what else will be changed, now that we've broken the bridge."

And now that Dexter's lost his power, he added silently. "First things first, I've got to go see my dad."

He didn't think of looking at his watch again till they were walking down the hill from the pine ridge. "Three-forty. We've only been away a few hours. At least nobody'll be worried about us."

"Right . . . " Fleur cocked her head. "What's that?"

Then he heard it too, a tangle of voices. And somebody was crying. The noise burst at them as they ducked through the gap in the lilac hedge. But it wasn't the noise that floored Neil.

"Oh, my good glory," Fleur breathed.

The tower had fallen. It lay in three sections, with crushed apple trees bristling through the gaps. The copper dome lay by itself, like a helmet knocked off a giant's head.

People crawled over and through the debris like ants. Neil wondered what they were looking for.

"Look, it's my dad!" Fleur said. "And my mom, and Betts, and oh, horrors, its the whole bunch!"

She grabbed up her skirts and ran toward the ruin. Neil raced after her. Somebody saw them and yelled, "There they are!" Somebody else screamed.

Then the garden was streaming with people, all running and shouting. Fleur was mobbed. Everybody was hugging her.

"My baby! We thought . . . "

" . . . under that wreck . . . "

"That dress! Where . . . "

" . . . a friend, Mom. I traded for it."

" . . . out of our minds!"

Neil backed away from the crowd, glad to escape un-mauled. He turned around and came face to face with Gregory. Whiter than usual. His teeth clenched. He looked as if he could take Neil's head off at one swipe.

"You're better!" Neil babbled, to give Gregory a chance to get a grip on himself. "They told me you'd be out of it for days. How come . . . " He faltered.

Gregory cleared his throat. "I woke up about an hour ago. I knew something had happened. Something . . . very wrong. The nurse told me there'd been an earth tremor."

"Tremor?" That breathless moment when Fleur set Dexter's world in motion. Even here they'd felt the shock wave.

"Nothing in the town was damaged. Just the tower, here. Then I couldn't find you, and the Padgetts couldn't find Fleur." He jerked his chin at the mob. "But one of the boys knew you'd come here. So we all thought . . . we thought you were under . . . "

"We were in the maze," Neil said quickly.

"So I see! I don't suppose you can tell me what you were doing there? Or who — " He stopped and they stared at each other.

Neil knew they were both thinking of the boy on the highway. The one who'd called himself Jasper.

"Well." Gregory looked away. "Maybe someday."

"Someday," Neil agreed. He drew a deep breath of relief.

"Come on," his father said. "Show you something."

They walked together past the broken sections of the tower, around to the front of the house. The Padgetts streamed after them like a comet, with Fleur rustling at the head in her brand-new antique dress and carrying Piglet in her arms. They were all still talking and laughing at once.

At first Neil saw no change in the house. Then Gregory pointed out the cracks that zigzagged from the foundation to the roofline.

"You won't get that patched up in a hurry," said Fleur's father. "That's fit to be bulldozed and nothing else."

Fleur's mother slipped an arm through Gregory's and squeezed. "And you'd just found a buyer. What a terrible loss!"

Neil's eyes met his father's. Gregory's smile was like a light behind his face.

"It's only money. There are more important things."

They never did go back in, not to bring out the furniture, not even to collect their clothes and suitcases. Gregory said it wasn't safe, that the house might collapse at any time. It turned out he was right.

Next day, when they came back with the demolition contractor, the only part left standing was the front right-hand corner with — miraculously unbroken — the beige marble staircase and the blue-and-gilt Moorish vase.

∞

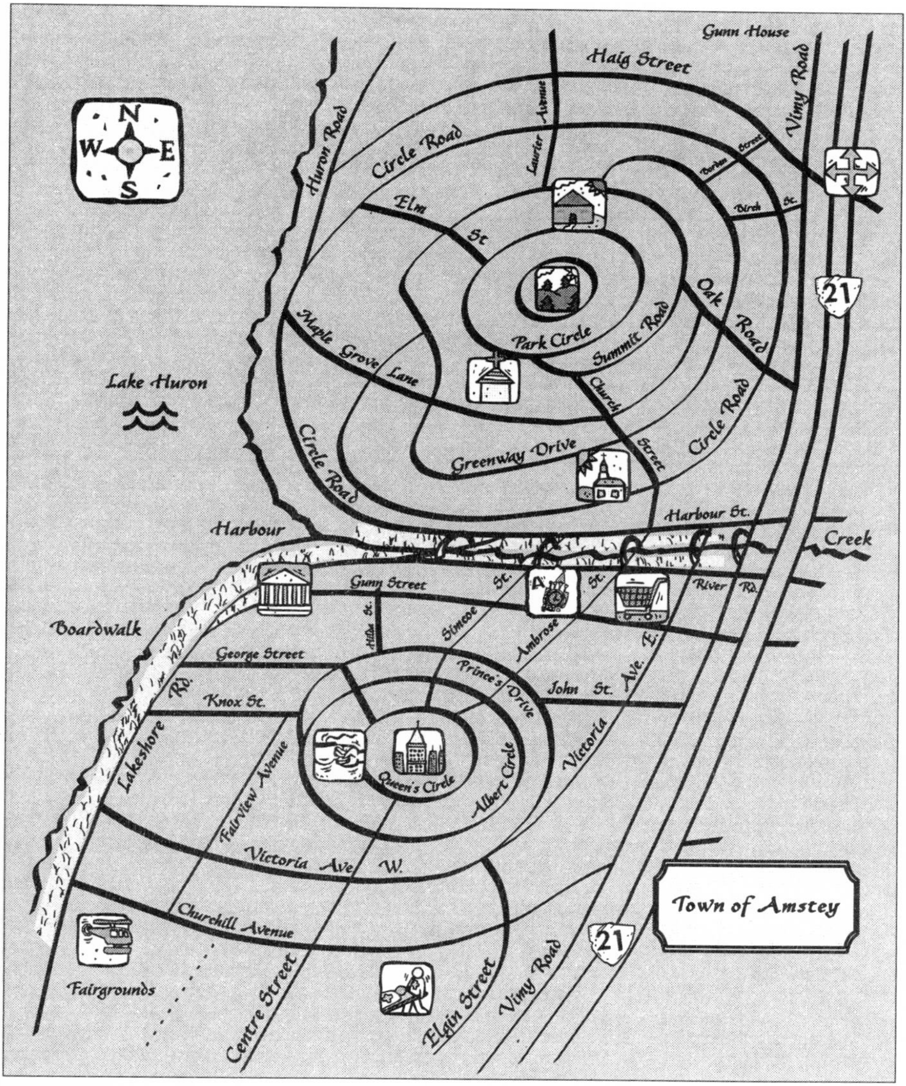
N
W
E
S
Gunn House
Haig Street
Vimy Road
Laurier Avenue
Huron Road
Circle Road
Borden Street
Birch St.
Elm St
21
Oak Road
Summit Road
Park Circle
Maple Grove Lane
Church Street
Lake Huron
Circle Road
Greenway Drive
Circle Road
Harbour St.
Harbour
Creek
Gunn Street
Simcoe St.
Ambrose St.
River Rd.
Hilda St.
Boardwalk
George Street
Prince's Drive
John St.
Victoria Ave. E.
Knox St.
Lakeshore Rd.
Fairview Avenue
Queen's Circle
Albert Circle
Victoria Ave. W.
Town of Amstey
Churchill Avenue
21
Fairgrounds
Centre Street
Elgin Street
Vimy Road

- City Hall
- Padgetts' Coffee Shop
- War Memorial
- Venables' Antiques
- Market
- Hospital
- Parkland
- Helicopter Pad
- Hilltop Park
- Padgetts' House
- St. Michael's Church
- Crossroad
- Knox Presbyterian Church

Printed in May 1997 by

in Boucherville, Quebec